Birds On A Wire Medica
120 Marketplace Circle
Suite C #362
Georgetown, KY 40324
www.birdsonawiremedia.com

For information for speaking events or interviews with the author go to:
georgiacurtisling.com

For Lauren
The woman my son married, and became
my lovely daughter-in-heart.

Contents

Copyright

Dedication

Chapter One   2

Chapter Two   14

Chapter Three   30

Chapter Four   45

Chapter Five   53

Chapter Six   65

Chapter Seven   76

Chapter Eight   87

Chapter Nine   91

Chapter Ten   102

Chapter Eleven   112

Chapter Twelve   124

Chapter Thirteen   132

Chapter Fourteen   145

Chapter Fifteen   155

Chapter Sixteen   165

Chapter Seventeen   175

Chapter Eighteen   186

Chapter Nineteen   193

Chapter Twenty   203

Chapter Twenty-One   215

Chapter Twenty-Two   226

Scripture Reference   232

About The Author   236

A *Christmas* BLESSING FOR *Gracie*

Sometimes we need a
divine intervention.

georgia curtis ling

A Spring Valley Heartwarming Romance
BOOK THREE

BIRDS ON A WIRE MEDIA

Through love serve one another.

A CHRISTMAS BLESSING FOR GRACIE

BY

GEORGIA CURTIS LING

©2023

Chapter One

F ive years. That's how long it had been since the accident and when the course of her life changed forever—when hopelessness moved in.

Five years ago, Courtney's happy life turned upside-down and became a world of misery. Love wasn't supposed to hurt. Love wasn't supposed to destroy. Love was supposed to love. Courtney just wanted life to be happy again. If she could only remember the good times. The bad seemed to muffle—smother the good memories.

For some time, the fear, helplessness, and endless turmoil put her and her children's lives on hold. Frozen in place. She'd felt unable to make plans for the future.

She had regrets. She regretted not reconnecting with her father sooner. She regretted not walking out the first time her husband pounded on her face with his fists. She regretted the emotional trauma her children endured. But she would never regret bringing life into this world. Even though their father had lost his way, her children were her saving grace.

As she neared the mailbox, Courtney stopped to take in the surroundings at the Ramsey homeplace. The enchanting mountains turned shades of blazing orange, red, gold, and brown, calling out-of-towners from all over the world to visit. She felt blessed that this was her home.

After she'd moved from Concord, North Carolina to Pikeville, Kentucky in Appalachia and became a mother, autumn became Courtney's favorite time for memory-making adventures with her children. She closed her eyes and breathed in fall's perfume. The earthy smell of fallen leaves as plants and nature hunkered down for the winter awakened her senses.

She'd spent most of October carrying out her Autumn Family Experience Checklist. She'd checked off most of their fall fun activities list— visiting the pumpkin patch, racking and playing with the kids in a pile of crunchy leaves, baking spice bread, and sipping apple cider. Tonight was the grand finale of the fall festivities. She valued the last few minutes of her morning walk and quiet-time before the mayhem moved in.

In the crisp air, she walked on, retrieved the mail and turned back toward the house that sat at the end of the long tree-lined driveway. In the distance, she could see her children with their grandfather, Papaw Rich, busy carving pumpkins on the porch. She smiled and watched as their feisty dog wanted to assist in the activity, but his short legs failed the attempted high jump on to the worktable. The excited little corgi's 'big dog' bark echoed down the drive. She wasn't crazy about the idea last Christmas when her dad bought the kids pets. Chance, her ten-year-old, was thrilled with his corgi puppy, whom his papaw had named Nick. Her eight-year-old daughter, Gracie, was smitten with her sweet, snow-white kitten christened Angel. Even though Courtney wasn't a fan of house pets, she had to admit Nick and Angel proved to be great emotional support for the kids —exactly what they needed.

Two years ago, she was physically, emotionally, and mentally exhausted. In the middle of a cold, snowy December, she and the kids were living in a shelter for abused women and children, and the only emotion she remembered feeling was hopelessness. Still, the kids kept her from abandoning the fight to survive. Then, an unforeseen light in her life—her rescuer—her father—arrived in the darkest moments, giving her a glimmer of hope.

The trouble began when Josh, her husband of seven years, fell off of a roof at work and injured his back. Months later, he recovered from the physical injury but not from the prescribed painkillers. They changed him. She didn't recognize the desperate man he'd transformed into. He wasn't a partner; he was a foe. He'd spend all their money on drugs. His verbal abuse led to physical abuse—sunglasses became the norm for her, even on cloudy days. She'd quit using her bank card because of the embarrassment of being declined, due to insufficient funds. So, she stashed cash, hidden away for groceries. The day she saw Josh digging through her purse for the designated grocery money to feed her children, she found herself in a scuffle with her husband. She tried to yank her purse away from him but lost the battle. He beat her—again. In a panic, while he was out in search of a fix, she packed a suitcase, took the children, and fled to Haven House. The shelter for abused women and children was three hours away in Spring Valley, Tennessee, and she hoped it would be far enough from him to provide security for her children. She'd prayed for a miracle.

Three weeks from Christmas, she and her children, gratefully settled in their own private room in the shelter. Her heavy-hearted family needed some joy in their lives, so on a whim, Courtney took them to Spring Valley's Santa Train Depot for holiday pictures. It turned out to be the beginning of a Christmas miracle.

Unbeknownst to Courtney, the local stand-in for Father Christmas was her estranged father, Rich Ramsey. The man she'd blamed for her mother's fatal car accident. The man she'd abandoned when she'd left home at the age of eighteen. The man she'd tried to erase from her life. The same man who ultimately became her rescuer.

In the course of time, Courtney learned that Rich became a changed man when he'd turned his life over to Christ and was twenty years sober. Her grandparents had passed, and their house was unoccupied. He'd offered Courtney the keys to the old farmhouse—with no strings attached. She accepted his generous offer, mainly because she wanted to give her children a safe place to call home.

As she reconnected with her father, she offered him forgiveness—the Christmas wish he'd prayed to receive for so many years. She'd come to rely on Rich and the arm of support extended from her new church family.

After she'd fled, her husband filed for divorce. Truth be told, if her father wasn't a good Christian man, he would have hunted Josh down and killed him. But he didn't; he didn't have to.

Just days after signing the divorce papers, Josh knew he needed another Percocet to feed his addition—to relieve his pain. What he didn't know was fentanyl had made its way into the smuggled counterfeit pill he'd purchased, and after swallowing the lethal dose, he would die in a matter of minutes. His bereaved mother called Courtney with the tragic news. That was the day fentanyl came for the father of her children.

Life wasn't supposed to be this hard, especially for her children. Chance, ever the protector, had proved to be resilient, but she worried Gracie's heart held the imprint of their troubled past. Shy and cautious, she wasn't as carefree as a little girl should be. She laughed and played, but genuine happiness seemed just beyond her reach—an elusive notion. Courtney hoped and prayed for a joy-giving holiday miracle for Gracie.

Courtney's wounded heart still needed healing, but she'd recognized a lightness in her spirit as her life seemed more back on track. When the storm calmed in her life, Courtney renewed her interest in pursuing a nursing career.

A few years earlier, with the nation-wide medical personnel shortage, she was recruited by her mother-in-law to become a certified nursing assistant with an incremental path to become an RN. She'd just started work at the hospital when her husband was injured and her life stalled. After settling in Tennessee, she found employment at the local medical center, and she anticipated a call this afternoon for details on a new assignment.

She didn't allow herself to relive the past years very often but sometimes the memories helped her see the fresh promises of God as he renews her heart daily. She refocused her mind on the house in front of her. Every time she admired her new home, she felt blessed. When her father offered Courtney her grandparents' house, she envisioned the modest farmhouse she visited as a child. When Rich picked them up at the shelter and drove to the farm, she was shocked at the site of their new home. They were greeted by a renovated and modern farmhouse, now painted in a glorious almond white color with timber columns, wood shutters, and board and batten siding. The welcoming wrap-around porch, complete with a porch swing and rocking chairs, invited her to relax and sit a spell. A two-car garage addition with carriage doors, gooseneck barn lights, and a guest studio apartment were unimaginable luxuries for a girl who just left a homeless shelter. It was the house of her dreams.

She'd never imagined that so much could change in a few short years. Nothing prepared her for the miracles that materialized. It had to have been a divine blessing—that was the only explanation she could fathom.

She walked the last few feet to the porch and plopped down in a rocking chair as Nick, the corgi, turned his attention toward her and began bouncing up and down on his short, springy legs, attempting to land in her lap. He succeeded. Courtney stroked the dog to calm him.

"Your pumpkins look great!" Courtney looked beyond the mess to the masterpieces. "Are you sure a professional carver didn't sneak in while I was gone and give you a little help?"

"No, I promise," Gracie assured her mother. "Cross my heart, I did it all by myself."

"Are you sure about that?" Her papaw tried to keep her honest.

"Well, you may have helped a little." With a sculpting tool in hand, Gracie stepped back to admire her handiwork. "The carving kit and stencils Papaw bought helped a lot." With a congratulatory grin, she added, "I think this is my best ever pumpkin—ever in a kazillion years!"

Courtney was surprised by her daughter's

choice. A traditional face with cut-out triangular eyes and nose with a monstrously grinning mouth. "You'll scare the trick-or-treaters away."

Gracie protested, "It's supposed to be scary!"

Courtney turned her attention to her son. "I love your buccaneer pumpkin."

Chance was putting the finishing touches on his pirate jack-o'-lantern. He'd carved one eye and found a magic marker to color a patch for the other and drew a line for the string. "Thanks, Mom. Do you have an old bandana scarf to wrap around the top of the pumpkin?"

"I'm sure we have one tucked away in a drawer. I'll look in a few minutes."

She examined the carving tools spread out on the table. "Dad, whatever happened to using your hand to scoop out the guts and a kitchen knife for carving? You're spoiling these kids."

"That's my job!" Rich took his papaw duties seriously and overindulged his grandkids whenever he could—at least, when his daughter would allow. He'd missed out on so many years, and he wanted to make as many memories with them as possible.

"Hon, would you be so kind as to bring me a cup of coffee?"

Courtney lifted the snoozing dog out of her lap and left him snoring on the comfy seat cushion. She headed to the kitchen to fetch her dad his coffee. On the way, she decided she could use a cup, too.

Courtney began her love affair with coffee on the morning of her thirteenth birthday when her mom welcomed her to the wonderful world of the dark brew. It was a gift. She remembered feeling so grown-up. Every morning after that first celebratory morning, they bonded over coffee —sometimes, they fought over coffee. She missed those mornings with Mom.

Coffee ran in the veins of both sides of her family. It must be why Courtney, just like Granny Ramsey, kept a pot brewing and warming on the back burner. The nutty aroma reminded her of walking into her granny's kitchen and feeling a warm welcome.

Standing in her grandmother's kitchen— hers now, Courtney felt content.

As she handed Rich his fresh brew, she reminded the kids of the time. "We've got to leave in about an hour to get to the inn to help Nana Alana hand out treats. You've got to clean up and gather your costumes for the costume contest. And don't forget Nick's garb. Let's hurry up."

Close to two years ago, Rich had met Alana at the Spring Valley Inn. When he was slammed with Santa appearances, for convenience, he'd decided to book a room during most of December. Little did he know, he'd share wedding vows with the innkeeper, in the courtyard of the inn, the follow summer. Courtney was happy her father had a second chance at love, and she and the kids absolutely adored Alana. Spring Valley held a special place in her dad's heart. It's where he found his daughter and met his love.

"Don't worry about their pumpkins. I'll bring them for the Jack-o'-Lantern Drive Thru on Main Street. I'll make sure they line up the kid's pumpkins in front of the inn," Rich volunteered, hoping to make the trip less stressful for his daughter. "When these orange guys get lit up, they are going to be eerie." He held one up in front of his face. "When you kids get tired of handing out treats at the inn, I'll walk you down Main Street, so you can trick-or-treat and see the display of jack-o'-lanterns." Rich loaded the pumpkins in his truck. Before driving away, he rolled down his window and offered, "If Chance wants to ride in with me, just drop him off at my house on the way out." Chance gave him the thumps up.

Chance and Gracie agreed to the plan as they rushed around with their cleaning tasks.

Before the pumpkin innards made their way to the trash, Courtney pointed to the baggies and reminded the carvers, "Hey, don't throw those away. Put them in a plastic bag and refrigerate. I'm going to dry and roast them."

"Yuck!" Gracie scrunched her face as she reluctantly scooped the goop into a bag. "I don't think I like pumpkin seeds."

"Hate to tell you, sweet pea, but you eat them all the time."

"No, I don't."

Chance jumped in the conversation. "Yes,

you do, Gracie, but you call them pepitas."

"I love pepitas!" Gracie licked her lips. "We can just buy them at the store." Doubting her mother's culinary skills. "Are you sure you can make them, Mom?"

"Granny used to say, 'Don't let anything go to waste.' I'm just trying to follow her advice. It'll be a family cooking project. If they're not edible, we'll feed them to the birds. How, bout it?"

"Only if I don't have to touch this goop again." Gracie was always the negotiator.

"Deal!" Courtney helped with the cleanup to speed the process. She felt as if she were herding cats. "Time's a wastin'. Let's get moving so we can get out of here, or you're going to miss out on a spooktacular time!"

Chance rolled his eyes. Gracie giggled. "Did you get it?" Gracie turned to her brother and sounded out, "Spook-tac-ular." Invading his space, she waved her arms in a ghostly flow.

"Mom, make her stop, or I'm going to scare the bejeebers out of her."

Hands on her hips, Courtney gave her final warning. "Last chance. I'll give you two a choice. We can stand here and pick at each other all night, or we can go have some fun at the Halloween Haunts and Happenings." Displeasure raised her eyebrows. "It's your call."

Her children buttoned up their lips and scurried off to their rooms to grab costumes.

She sighed, gathered her purse, phone, keys,

and the dog's leash. It was only two in the afternoon. She was curious if the evening held any more *spooktacular* surprises.

With her kids, only time would tell.

Just as they buckled their seat belts, her cell phone rang. She recognized the number and debated with herself, whether or not to take the call. On the third ring, she unbuckled, and stepped out of the car to answer the phone.

Chapter Two

By three in the afternoon, Blake had arrived at the inn, registered, and received his room access card. Thus far, he'd give the Spring Valley Inn five stars. The charming hotel was located in the middle of a lively, tree-lined historic downtown district that gave off an artsy-crafty kind of vibe. He'd always preferred boutique inns over booking a recognizable brand name. Being away from home for nine months out of the year, he'd found the small inns cozy and welcoming. The friendly receptionist provided tips on where to shop and dine as well as information on the guided historic walking tour. She'd guaranteed it would be the perfect way to be immersed in the beauty and history of Spring Valley. In the spirit of the season, she also highly recommended the spooky cemetery tour where, from time-to-time, ghosts were known to make appearances.

His accommodations reminded him of a mini-version of the lavish Biltmore Inn in Asheville, North Carolina, where he'd attended a family wedding. He could tell the room had been recently renovated with décor that gave it a touch of elegance. The bed was dressed in luxurious linens. The pillows looked firm and inviting. He'd spent many nights sleeping on whatever worn out pillow was available on a missionary medical tour. Just by looking, he could tell he would be comfortably dreaming tonight.

The personalized service was appealing—he liked feeling special, and he particularly liked the outstanding, freshly-baked, oatmeal cookies available at the hospitality table in the lobby as they added a delicious touch. He looked forward to the gourmet breakfast offered by their award-winning chef. To top it off, he'd managed to negotiate a great rate for his extended three-month stay. He'd found the manager more than willing to work out an amicable deal.

The sudden screech of steel against steel demanded his attention. The sticking and slipping of train wheels bumping over the tracks, followed by jarring blasts of a whistle, meant the rail lines were close—very close. As a young boy, Blake associated the piercing sound with a feeling of adventure. As a man, in search of a sound sleep, he hoped there were no night trains.

He pushed back the window curtain to survey. From his second-story view, he noticed an appealing shop only a short walk up the hill. Blake eyed the Mockingbird Coffee House. It was the first coffee shop on the list the receptionist provided and personally gave high praise. The railroad tracks, noisy and snug between a Federal-style home and the coffee house, was idyllic. With the steady stream of customers that he spied going in and out, it must be worth the walk for a brew. He'd spent the last seven hours driving, and he could use another caffeine boost to carry him through to lights out.

The trip wasn't as harried as some travels he'd made in the last two years. Driving his own vehicle eliminated the frustrations and stresses of traveling by plane. He'd lost count of the number of times delayed flights left him worrying if he'd make his connection to his final destination. Travel delays were the bane of his road-warrior existence. If he'd had his own plane, life would be much simpler. But that and other unrealistic wishes were not granted. Maybe, he decided, he needed a more practical wish list.

Blake hated not being in control, and everything was out of his control at an airport. During the delays, he'd learned to settle in, check emails, review tasks for his next assignment, or catch up on the latest medical journal. At least, when he was behind the wheel of his own Jeep, he felt more in control of his circumstances—even if it was a false perception.

While traveling, Blake liked to unpack as soon as he arrived. It made his room feel homey and organized. He'd admit on the scale between crazy-off-the wall neat freak and slob, he was closest to crazy-off-the-wall. Structure came in handy in his sometimes-chaotic profession. He'd found that organized medical offices tended to operate more efficiently, which allowed him to be more productive.

He'd become a champion minimalist packer. It wasn't too difficult for him since his work wardrobe consisted of medical scrubs. Jeans, casual shirts, hoodies, and workout gear filled most of his luggage. He'd thrown in a dressy shirt, just in case a special event required him to dress up his jeans. He pulled the last few pieces out of his suitcase. The writing desk gave him ample space for his workstation where he organized his art supplies.

Providing his own transportation allowed extra space to bring along personal items for the "me" ways he liked to spend his private time.

During medical training, he was encouraged to nurture his passion. Besides medicine, his passion was art, and watercolor was his favorite medium. A paintbrush in his hand had a calming effect as lines, colors, shapes, and shadows brought life to paper. Away from the daily stress, his creative art work made him feel happier.

On the beach in the Outer Banks, when he was eight-years-old, his grandmother first introduced him to her beautiful world of watercolor. He recalled the first time he'd helped her drag her portable painting easel over the sand dunes. His toes and the wheel of the utility wagon sank deep in the sand as he followed her, searching for the perfect breathtaking spot on the beach. She always said that art revealed a bit of her soul that told a story. Her captivating art—her storytelling, reflected the natural beauty of the Outer Banks and the common folk who called it home. She brought the coastlines to life. When he looked at her beach landscapes, he could feel the strong breeze as it bent the tall sea oats guarding the sand dunes as it lifted a gull that floated against a clear sky. She had him hooked on art. In his teens, surfing and sailing became another passion, but aquatic hobbies were limited by location. He could take a few essential art supplies anywhere in the world.

He stowed his suitcase under the bed. With heavy eyes, he contemplated a nap, but instead, he chose to visit the coffee house on the hill.

***

Blake sat enjoying his coffee in the corner booth of the upper level of the coffee house. He enjoyed the bird's eye view taking in the magnificent architecture of the old church building.

A woman approached with a dessert, that he didn't order, and slid it in front of him.

"I'm Ada Taylor, the owner of this fine establishment. I like to introduce myself to newcomers in town."

"Nice to meet you, Ada. I'm Blake Boone visiting from North Carolina." He pointed to the cake. "I think you have the wrong table. It looks delicious, but I didn't order it."

"I know you didn't. This is an apple stack cake; I'm thinking about adding it to the menu. If you want to try it and let me know what you think, it's on the house."

"Absolutely, I'm not that hungry, but I can force myself." Force would not be required. He couldn't imagine anyone would turn down the five-layered cake.

"It's an old-timey recipe here in Appalachia. Back in the day, for wedding cakes, neighbors pitched in and brought a spiced molasses cake layer, then the mother-of-the-bride would add the filling. It has a spicy apple butter filling, perfect for fall weather. I thought it would go well with our pumpkin latte."

As he lifted his fork for the first bite, Ada slid into the seat across from him to get better acquainted. Blake didn't realize the cake came with conversation.

"Are you staying down at the inn?" Ada thought she'd start with small talk before she heard what she really wanted to hear.

"Yes, I just checked in this afternoon. I'm impressed with the accommodations."

"That little hotel is something else, alright. You know, it's survived three fires. Back in the late 1800s, almost every wood structure on Main Street burned to the ground. It's a miracle the inn is still standing. In recent years, when sweet Robin, God rest her soul…"

When Ada touched her hand to her heart, Blake knew a sad story followed.

"When she inherited the inn from her grandparents, Robin and her newlywed husband,

Gabe—now he's a looker! Yes, they ran the inn together, until she passed from cancer."

He concluded he wasn't going to get a word in edgewise, so Blake took another bite of the heavenly spice cake. It was like a fall festival for his taste buds. He listened as Ada rambled on.

"Gabe tried inn-keeping alone, but after a couple of years when he met and fell in love with a local girl, Shauna, he sold the inn to his mother, Chef Jean, and his Aunt Alana. They were semi-retired looking for an adventure and boy, did they ever find it!

Blake screamed in his head, *"Oh, my gosh, lady, couldn't you have just handed me a pamphlet?"*

But Ada continued her chat. "Alana fell in love and married one of their guests. Their wedding was in the courtyard."

Blake was waiting for the full description of the wedding gown, but it never came. Ada moved her tour to the courtyard.

"And, oh my, that English garden courtyard is breathtaking…"

He wondered if she would ever take a breath. She had the lungs of a whale. Anytime, he expected a spray of water to spring from the top of her head when she surfaced for air.

"In spring and summer, people come from all over to get married there." She took a breath. "You married?" She didn't stop for Blake's reply. From the town's grapevine, she knew the answer before she asked. "You chose a very romantic inn.

Must be fate."

"You never know." Blake quipped.

Ada ignored him. She knew all about fate, and as a matter of fact, she was sizing him up for a potential match in her unofficial role as the town matchmaker.

"Lordy, lordy, I've blabbed until your ears look sore. I haven't let you get a word in edgewise." She sat back in the booth and made herself comfortable. "Tell me a little about yourself. What brings you to our neck of the woods?"

He concluded not only was she a fast talker, she was also a mind reader.

Blake questioned his coffee run decision. He didn't want to be rude, but she was exhausting. He had to admit, though, there was something extraordinary about this sweet, plumpish, grandmotherly lady. She was definitely entertaining and friendly. Was it her delicious dessert or the glimmer in her dark brown eyes that made her so delightful?

"I'm a travel nurse practitioner. I'll be working with the hospital filling in for the NP on maternity leave."

That's what Ada wanted to hear. "Oh, really. I have a young friend, Courtney. She's about your age and works at the hospital. I'll have her look you up."

"Actually, I won't be in the hospital. I'm the NP for the mobile clinic. Every day, I'll be out in rural areas serving clients. Odds are, we would never meet." Blake stood to leave. "By the way, the apple stack cake was incredible."

"Before you leave, get a coffee to-go. It's on the house. Tell them Ada sent you." Ada scooted her way out of the booth. When she tried to stand, she felt a tinge dizzy and wobbled. She surmised she'd sat too long. Blake put his hand on her back to give Ada support.

"Bless your heart, my achy knees are screaming at me." She balanced herself then patted him on the back. "Thanks for being my taste tester. You come back and see me."

Ada cleared the table as Blake made his way down the stairs. She had a track record of improving the odds. She had a hunch she'd found the ideal candidate for Courtney, but bringing them together might be an ambitious assignment. The Lord had guided her paths with the last two successful matchmaking attempts, and she'd call on the Lord one more time. Ada always thought she and her Maker made a good team.

***

The afternoon sun was warm on his face when he stepped outside the coffee house. He noticed the blessing posted over the door, *The Lord bless thee, and keep thee*. While waiting on his to-go drink, he read a plaque on the wall and learned that the coffee house was a former "1871 Greek Revival majestic house of worship." The stunning stained-glass windows cast a heavenly light throughout the coffee house. He'd felt as if he'd been to church.

If the Mockingbird Coffee House and its owner, Ada, were an example of the town's hospitality, he had a good feeling about Spring Valley.

Fall leaves swirling in the wind covered the sidewalk. Costumed urchins merged on the town for the annual Haunts and Happenings costume contest and trick-or-treating in downtown Spring Valley. A little jailbird, dressed in black and white stripes, hurried passed Blake, gripping a vintage canvas Barkley's Bank money bag to gather his treats. Blake drifted back into his memory and felt a smack of sadness.

The last Halloween he'd celebrated at a Boos and Brews celebration in Nags Head was where his ex-fiancé, Karen, broke their engagement. She'd insisted on dressing up in matchy-matchy costumes. It didn't matter to Blake; he was just going for the brews. She bought the cutesy costumes online. He didn't know if it was subliminal or not, but she chose the traditional black and white striped prisoner costume with a ball a chain. They'd turned a few heads that evening on the beach, but not for their creative attire. Sometime during the bash, he didn't remember exactly how it came about, but during a silly spat, she shouted to the whole world that she didn't want to be sentenced to life in a marriage with him. She threw the plastic ball and chain at him first; the gigantic diamond engagement ring followed, which left a mark on his face. Then his ex-prison mate stormed off into the night.

Two years ago, at that Halloween party, life took on a new direction for Blake. Disillusioned in the matters of love, he declared himself officially off the market, swore he would never again date a co-worker, and redirected his career to travel nursing. As a nurse practitioner, he was in high demand. After acquiring an agency, within weeks he jumped into his first assignment and never looked back.

As Blake opened the inn's door and stepped inside, a little girl being pulled by a rambunctious corgi ran through the entrance with Blake directly in their path. She was a carbon copy of the beautiful woman trailing behind the girl and her dog. The child's chestnut-colored hair with fringy bangs was pulled back in a ponytail, flopping back and forth as quickly as her dog's short and fluffy wagging tail.

She squealed when almost in an instant, the yelping dog ran in circles around Blake and bound his feet together with the leash. With his coffee in one hand, Blake tried to stay upright by balancing with his arms, but it was futile. His drink went flying and plopped smack dab in the middle of the embossed entryway rug. Before the mother could completely disentangle the dog's hostage, Blake managed to grab the stair handrail to keep from crushing her, and her look-alike, in an impending fall. Miraculously, Blake landed on the stairs as the mother wriggled the dog free.

Through her nervous giggle, the little girl

informed him, "You looked like a surfer." In spite of all the excitement, the corgi stopped and watched his human playmate as she imitated Blake's surfing-balance move.

"I've been on a surf board a time or two." Unamused by the embarrassing situation, his frustrated frown slowly grew to a polite grin as he picked himself up off the floor.

Surveying the situation, the little girl's eyes widened. Anxious to avoid a reprimand, she offered a quick '*sorry*' and raced off to the kitchen with her furry companion, leaving her mom behind to present an official apology to the stranger and clean up the mess.

"I am so sorry." The beautiful mom wanted to laugh, but held back. "Are you okay?"

"My ego is wounded, but I'll survive."

She picked up the paper coffee cup and noticed the Mockingbird Coffee House logo. "What did you have to drink? I'll run to the coffee house for a replacement."

Blake objected to the kind gesture. "No, that's completely unnecessary. It was just black coffee. Fortunately, there were only a few sips left which kept it from being a total disaster."

She smiled at him, hoping to lighten the mood of the unfortunate mishap.

"There's no such thing as 'just' coffee," she enlightened him. "Coffee is the nectar of life."

She stepped a few feet away, hurriedly grabbed a handful of napkins from the hospitality tray, and began dabbing up the mess. "The tornado that swept through here is my daughter, Gracie. The feisty little corgi's name is Nick. She is overly excited to help her nana hand out Halloween treats tonight at the inn. As you can tell, she lets her excitement get the best of her. When you add the corgi in the mix, it gets doubly entertaining."

The dog's bark echoing from the kitchen interrupted their conversation. "Chef Jean doesn't allow dogs in her work space. Excuse me, but I'm needed." As she pushed open the swinging kitchen door, she turned to face him. "Are you sure you don't want a replacement? It will only take a minute for a coffe run."

"I'm good. Go rescue the chef!" Blake assured her as he watched her disappear through the door.

It wasn't his intent, but he was sure he came across as irritated. Embarrassment had a way of revealing his testy side. If he ever encountered them again, he'd be sure to be on his best behavior. He was also a little bummed out for not making formal introductions. She walked away, and he didn't know the woman's name.

***

Exasperated with her daughter, she shook her head wondering how many fires she would have to put out in the next few hours. Courtney hoped there wouldn't be any real fires.

She found Gracie frozen in her footsteps watching Chef Jean, with wooden spoon in hand, scolding Nick. He sat petrified on his hind legs in quiet obedience—Courtney was confident he'd turned to stone from pure terror. When corgi Nick met Chef Jean, he met his alpha human. Courtney decided she needed to go on bended knee and beg Chef Jean to consider serving as the obedience trainer for Nick.

***

When Rich arrived with Chance and the jack-o'-lanterns, Courtney made a mad dash to the coffee house to replace the grumpy guest's drink. She asked the receptionist for his room number, made her way to the second floor, and gently knocked on his door. "Room service."

He hadn't ordered room service. Through the door's peephole, Blake saw the gorgeous woman who'd freed him from the dog's leash. She held a take-out coffee cup. He ran his fingers through his mussed-up hair and then turned the door knob.

When he opened the door, she realized how exceptionally good-looking he was. He had hair the color of wheat with short and shaggy, sun-streaked layers, styled just between messy and casual. Unlike his earlier grouchy expression, his mouth held a slow smile—more relaxed and welcoming. His smokey gray eyes bore a resemblance to storm clouds and, she sensed, held a hint of loneliness. His tanned skin revealed he'd recently spent time where it was warm and sunny. She guessed he'd been on a surfboard more than a time or two.

"I know you said there was no need, but I just had to buy a replacement. Consider it an apology in a cup." She handed him the coffee and officially introduced herself. "I'm Courtney Clark."

"Seriously, you didn't have to, but apology accepted." Just what he'd hoped for—her name. He raised his drink in an imaginary toast. "Nice to meet you, Courtney. I'm Blake Boone."

"Nice to meet you. I won't be a pest and take up any more of your time. Hope you enjoy your stay."

Intriguing woman, Blake mused. He watched as she walked down the hallway, glanced over her shoulder, smiled, and waved.

She didn't notice if he waved back, but she did notice he wasn't wearing a wedding ring—not that it mattered. She just surprised herself that she deliberately looked.

Though friends and family gently encouraged her to give love a second chance, Courtney wasn't ready to open her wounded heart to another. She'd enjoyed the attention of one guy, in particular, from her small group at church. She'd even ventured out on several enjoyable dates with him, but the relationship never progressed beyond friendship. Not because he'd lost interest; on the contrary, he was smitten with Courtne. Yet, she was not ready to commit. He gave up and moved on. She remained in limbo—somewhere between loss and the intention of love.

She wondered if noticing was a sign that her

heart was on the mend.

Chapter Three

Courtney wasn't a beneficiary of a large insurance payout from her ex-husband's death. The night she fled with her children; she was flat broke. Except for the few nickels, dimes, and quarters from her son's piggy bank she'd jammed in her luggage, she had nothing. She had to work. She wanted to work. She felt insecure with her new assignment, but she had to push through. She needed the money.

Her father was wealthy in his own right, and wanted to provide for her family, but she didn't want him to be her personal bank. He'd even provided transportation. Courtney wondered if when her dad purchased the Ford Escape for her, did he subconsciously choose the model because of its name? He'd provided a vehicle of escape from her tumultuous past. The topic of the car choice never surfaced. She'd accepted his generosity, but only until she got back on her feet. She'd suffered a difficult setback, but she was an adult woman and had the skills to survive.

Her dad and his wife, Alana, were her life support. Finding love after fifty, they were officially still considered newlyweds, but they willingly pitched in by caring for the kids after school, preparing snacks, and helping with homework until Courtney returned home from work. They were sensitive to the children's time of enduring hardship that would break a grown adult, and these grandparents loved them through the charged, emotional days that sneaked up on Chance and Gracie without warning. At the end of the day, Courtney and the kids knew they were loved, reminding Courtney she wasn't alone.

In the solitude of her car, she spoke her blessings out loud as she drove into work. She had a good job. A rent-free, beautiful home. She had her father back in her life and a confidant in Alana. A support system through church. Loyal friends. Chance made the honor roll and was awarded student of the week. Gracie continued to make new friends at school—she even smiled more.

Everything moved forward—except Courtney's love life. She'd consciously decided not to pursue a romantic relationship, but there was a problem with this plan. She was lonely and longed for companionship. She longed for love. She was young, and she wanted to share the rest of her life with someone. But her someone didn't have a name—yet.

Her someone may just be one of her illusive dreams. He'd have to love her children. Love and accept her, along with the scars of her past. He'd have to be kindhearted and a man of faith. It seemed to Courtney that if she were to ever meet the someone she desired, it would have to be a divine appointment.

She was ten minutes early when she pulled into the hospital's back parking lot. She saw the mobile medical bus and pulled into the closet available space. The bus was easy to spot because it was branded with a vinyl vehicle wrap that transformed a plain white exterior to a mobile billboard with bold colors and a life-size graphic of a woman holding her baby at a clinic visit. "Health Bus" was printed in giant letters across the top.

She noticed puffs of water vapors swirling around the exhaust pie as the engine idled. She panicked with the thought of being late. Did she forget the arrival time? She received the call from the HR Department with details for hew new assignment when she was leaving the house, on the way to the Halloween festivities, so she didn't write down the information. She prides herself in her ability to remember the smallest detail. Had she made a mistake? Was she supposed to arrive at seven-thirty instead of eight?

Like a whirlwind, she jammed everything in her backpack, even her soft lunch bag. As she flung it over her shoulder, she hoped nothing would spill. With her giant-sized insulated Yeti coffee tumbler in hand, she exited her car.

This was not her idea of making a good first impression.

***

Blake had spent all day Sunday in orientation meetings at the hospital. He came away feeling secure in his new leadership role and was ready for this three-month assignment. The healthcare outreach program in the mobile health clinic would be an exciting new adventure.

There were ups and downs for a traveling nurse practitioner, that was to be expected. But when challenged, Blake thrived. It afforded him the opportunity to explore working in different settings—especially, the underserved regions. Networking with physicians and administrators across the world gave him a broader base for referrals for future job opportunities, and the higher salary was extremely enticing.

Single, he didn't find it challenging to spend long periods of time away from his home base in Nags Head, North Carolina. In between assignments, he lived in his parents' guest house, not far from the beach. As an independent contractor, there were headaches involved with booking travel arrangements and short-term leases, but he managed. At first, he tried a staffing agency to book his travels, but more often than not, they booked boring hotels. When he took the task upon himself, he liked the hunt for the perfect hotel, one that celebrated the local culture. Working in multiple states, he relied on his CPA to estimate how much he would owe in federal and state income taxes—but as they say, *in this world nothing is certain, except death and taxes.* In his world, he'd add, *the certainty of health and malpractice insurance.* Thus far, the pros outweighed the cons. Life was good.

Monday morning, Blake arrived at the hospital at seven. A representative from the hospitals' Fleet Management department wanted to give him a quick tutorial on driving that specific bus. When he accepted the assignment, the hospital sent him to a driving bootcamp for commercial driver's licenses and special training for maneuvering large vehicles. Blake was surprised that driving the bus wasn't any harder than towing a large boat trailer, with which he had plenty of experience. After a few tense moments during his training, he mastered the wheel cut and pivot point. His driving skills made the task of learning easy. The most important reminder he'd received that morning was to give himself plenty of room while on the road and parking the rig, especially in the rural mountain area.

Twice, he'd warmed his cup of coffee in the mini-microwave, waiting for the nursing assistant to arrive.

He assumed the woman dressed in teal scrubs, sprinting toward the bus was the woman he was looking for.

She appeared as if she just woke up, ran a brush through her hair and walked out the door —not the frazzled, I don't care look—but rather a natural, effortless beauty. Her fringy bangs fell between her eyebrows and eyelashes, framing her hazel eyes. Blake took in every facet of her personal appearance. She looked familiar, but he didn't recall seeing her at yesterday's orientation meeting. He ate lunch in the hospital cafeteria; maybe he saw her there. Maybe he was just imagining they'd met because she would definitely leave an impression.

He smiled when she knocked on the passenger door. *It was a bus, no need to knock.*

"Come on board." He spoke loud enough for her to hear.

She pulled the door open and climbed up in the passenger seat like an old pro. She didn't bother to look his way. She was busy with her apology tour as she picked up the printed manual in the passenger seat, dumped her backpack at her feet, and slid her tumbler into the cup holder.

"I'm so sorry I'm late. I thought I was supposed to be here at eight." She strapped in the comfy captain's chair. "Otherwise, I would have been fifteen minutes early."

As soon as she spoke, he'd remembered where they met.

"You're the woman whose dog attacked me Saturday night."

She turned to get a clear picture of the driver and immediately recognized the handsome man behind the wheel. "Blake?"

He thought it a good sign that she'd remembered his name.

"Yes, Blake Boone, at your service."

"So, you're the nurse practitioner?" She looked surprised. "I didn't recognize you in scrubs."

"I'm assuming you're the nursing assistant?"

"Yes, I don't know if you remembered my name, I'm Courtney Clark."

Of course, he remembered her name. It had been swirling around in his head since they'd met at the inn.

"I assumed you were an employee at the inn since you seemed right at home."

"No, but it might as well be our second home. We spend most weekends at the inn. My father's wife, Alana, which you've probably met, is co-owner. The kids love visiting and from time-to-time, I'll help out when they're shorthanded."

Holding the manual close to her chest, she confessed, "I'm a little nervous. My new title, Community Health Navigator, is intimidating. It's a last-minute assignment for me. I'm the substitute for the employee that broke her leg over the week-end. I understand you're filling in for the nurse practitioner on maternity leave. I guess we're two peas in a pod." She paused to catch her breath. "And by the way, Nick, that's the dog's name, didn't attack, you just got tangled in his leash. And if you remember, I apologized profusely and replaced your coffee."

He surmised she talked too much when she was nervous. He thought it endearing. One of his sisters, when distressed, spoke a mile a minute, aimlessly babbling until her anxious sensations passed.

She outstretched her trembling hand. "I may need something to calm my nerves." She was half joking.

Blake didn't want to interrupt her, so he waited a few more seconds to jump in.

"If you're ready, I'll put this rig in drive. I'll admit, I'm a little nervous driving this for the first time." He wasn't the least bit nervous. He just wanted Courtney to not feel alone in her anxiety. "We'll take our time and drive slowly. GPS will be our guide."

The exterior of the Health Bus reminded Courtney of the coach motorhome her father owned when he traveled the NASCAR circuit. The inside was nothing like the luxury coach; instead, it was as expected—clinical. She turned in her seat in order to get a better view. To her left, patients would enter through a door that led directly to a tiny reception area with elbow-to-elbow booth seating, a built-in desk and chair for registration, and a compact work station. She was thrilled to see the Keurig K-Café coffee maker. Life was too short for bad coffee. She preferred drip coffee, but because the pods would be convenient, she wouldn't have to lug around her giant-sized coffee tumbler. Down the narrow hallway she could see an enclosed exam room, a private consultation room for blood draw, and a small restroom. The Health Bus reflected the mission of the hospital —transforming health care beyond hospital walls.

Pretty cool, she thought, that she had the privilege to serve in this way.

***

Blake took the interstate for a few miles to his exit. The secondary route with its twists and turns on narrow mountain roads were less than perfect driving conditions—especially, with a rookie behind the wheel. He managed to focus on the road and simultaneously carry on a conversation.

The drive was spent in medical jargon and delegating tasks and responsibilities. When Courtney first eyed the manual, sitting on the passenger seat, she took it as a sign that Blake meant business. Between Blake filling her in on the orientation meeting, one she'd wished she'd been asked to attend, and Courtney reviewing her manual, their driving time has no room for chit-chat. They arrived at their assigned location—a country church with a full parking lot.

Blake glanced at Courtney. Her mouth gaped open, and her eyes widened.

"Oh, my gosh, I knew it wasn't going to be an ordinary day at the clinic, but I didn't expect this." She didn't mean to say it out loud. She didn't want Blake to think she was terrified.

Courtney noticed a portable sign near the lot's entrance printed in large red letters, APPOINTMENT SLOTS ARE FILLED FOR TODAY. COME BACK TOMORROW. The words signaled their jam-packed day at the clinic.

"Looks like we're popular. Don't let the

crowd intimidate you. We'll do fine." Blake tried to keep her from panicking.

"It's too late for that." She was already wondering what she'd gotten herself in to.

From experience, Blake knew there would be nothing ordinary in the process of providing care for the underserved in isolated areas. But this was miniscule compared to when he'd volunteered on the Africa Mercy Ship for three months. On screening days, thousands of people in need of health care waited in line, and hundreds started forming lines the previous night. Today would be a walk in the park—he hoped.

During orientation, they warned Blake that patients arrived early. What he didn't know was how early. By seven that morning, a volunteer from the church had already distributed entry numbers as patients arrived, seeking free health care. The cut-off was twenty. If you were assigned the last number, you waited in your car or a designated room in the church until three o'clock. You could leave, but you'd risk losing your spot if you were late. Volunteers would go from car-to-car to distribute water bottles and snacks.

It only took fifteen minutes for the clinic to be up and running. By nine o'clock, Courtney greeted her first patient, a frail elderly woman.

"Well, aren't you the cutest little thing." The woman smiled at Courtney as she entered the bus. "I'm plumb tuckered out. My granddaughter got me here by six this morning. I didn't want to chance not gettin' in."

"Bless your heart, honey." Courtney took the woman by the arm and escorted her to a seat. "What's your name, sweet lady?"

"Ethel Bird." Her hands had a slight tremor. "I'm in that computer, somewhere. I've been here before."

"You're right, sweetheart. Your name popped right up."

From down the hallway in the exam room, Blake heard Courtney's syrupy language and couldn't keep from smiling. He wondered if she coated everything in sugar. He felt slighted because he'd been in her presence for several hours, and she hadn't referred to him as honey, sugar, or sweetie.

"Mrs. Bird, what brings you in today?" Courtney glanced over her patient's medical history. "Do you have your ID and any type of insurance card? If you don't have insurance, there's no worries. We provide free healthcare."

"I've just been feeling so poorly, lately. I can barely get out of bed. I reckoned I better get in to see if my ticker is okay. I've had heart ailments before." She thumbed through her wallet. "Here's my ID and Medicaid card if that helps."

"That's perfect." She scanned the cards and handed them back to Mrs. Bird. "I think that's all I need. Let's go down this hallway, and I'll introduce you to the nurse practitioner, Blake Boone. He met them halfway and greeted Mrs. Bird. Courtney returned to her computer to double check her work.

By noon, Blake was ready for a short break. Courtney chose to eat lunch in the bus, while Blake decided to stretch his legs and breathe in some fresh air. He grabbed his bagged lunch and walked outside as the sunshine peeked through the cloudy sky. He eyed a picnic table under an outdoor shelter, behind the church building. One of the volunteers had the same idea as Blake.

"Do you care if I join you?" Blake asked before seating himself.

"Have a seat." He looked up and introduced himself, "I'm, John, and I'd enjoy the company."

He sat across from the man who wore a blue and gold East Tennessee State Buccaneers cap. Blake guessed John was in his seventies. "I'm Blake, the nurse practitioner. Thank you for volunteering for the clinic." Blake unzipped the baggie to see what Chef Jean prepared for his lunch. He wasn't disappointed.

"It's my pleasure. The Lord willing, I'll be right here every time the mobile clinic rolls in."

"If I may be so bold to ask, what caused you to volunteer?"

"I'm seventy-two, a Tennessee native, and a retired dentist who grew up in this area. I'm a grandson of a coal miner and a proud alumnus of ETSU." He tipped his ballcap. "When I read online that the Health Bus would provide care in our community and needed volunteers, I had some free time on my hands, so I was one of the first to step forward."

"From the looks of the parking lot this morning, our services are needed." The sounds of music, talking, and a child that couldn't stop crying carried from vehicles as patients waited their turn. It made Blake want to rush through lunch to hurry back to seeing patients. It didn't seem to faze his dining-mate.

"Absolutely! We were hard-hit when coal-mining collapsed and are still struggling to rebuild our economy. It threw this region into economic distress and poor health. When folks have to choose between buying insurance or keeping the lights on and putting food on the table, they'll choose electric and groceries every time." He unwrapped what looked to be a homemade brownie. "I'm hoping that we get access to a mobile dental clinic in the near future. I've seen firsthand in my practice that folks can't afford dental care. They'll get a tooth ache, live on pain killers and tough it out, but eventually, they'll end up losing that tooth." He took a big bite of his dessert. "And let me tell you, when you lose a tooth, not only does it affect your self-esteem, but it affects your marketability and becomes tough to secure employment."

"I'll ask around and see when a dental bus will be available."

On the other side of the church building, Blake noticed additional parking that had four trailers set up. "What's with the travel trailers? Looks like a campground over there."

"Did you not hear about the flood that hit six months ago? Sixteen inches of rain fell in twenty-four hours. It just about washed this area off the face of the earth. We lost forty-five precious souls that day."

"That's tragic. I wasn't aware. I was out of the country on a medical mission trip, and I didn't keep up with the news in the states."

"Well, you're not the only one unaware. Since the news coverage moved on to the next big story, the rest of the world forgot about us, too. Around here, most are still living in survival mode."

John took a break from eating to tell the story. "There are bigger campgrounds filled with FEMA travel trailers, but the government didn't approve all the applications. These four families fell through the cracks and were denied temporary housing. One family was denied because their property was classified as a flood zone."

"That sounds ludicrous."

"I know, don't that beat all? We had one family from the church trapped in the holler for over a week. When the creek rose so fast, they knew they were in trouble and hiked their family up to higher ground. They watched as flood waters lifted their home off the foundation and floated down the creek. A bridge washed out; trees covered the road. It took several days for clearing crews on ATVs to rescue the family."

"They must have been terrified," Blake empathized.

"They were traumatized, all right. To make matters worse, they and three other families in our church were denied temporary housing. That's when our church decided that praying wasn't enough, and we had to do something. We pulled together our resources, found a compassionate soul who sold us the travel trailers at manufacturer cost, and set up our little camping ground, as you called it." He picked up his can of Dr. Enuf and took a drink. "The Bible says that God doesn't miss anything, and he won't forget the work we do by helping his needy people. It shows the love we have for him, and we need to keep at it."

"That's a good part of the reason I do what I do," Blake confessed.

"Keep it up, son. There's a whole lot more work that needs to be done."

"Amen, to that." Blake finished his short lunch. "Enjoyed meeting you, John. Thanks again for helping make this clinic possible."

"I'll be seeing you around."

Chapter Four

After his lunch break, Blake opened the door to the bus. The air smelled of lavender, fields and fields of lovely purple blooms.

"Is it my imagination, or did you just spray an entire can of air freshener?"

"I was attempting to freshen up the close quarters." She fanned the air with a folder. "I may have gone a little overboard."

"A little? How about a lot? We need to open the cab windows before we choke to death." Blake tapped the switch to control the power windows.

"Don't you think you're being a little dramatic? I found the freshener in the cabinet. I was glad whoever bought it chose the lavender scent. It's a sweet floral scent, and it has a way of relaxing and calming nerves." She'd hoped it would calm her nerves. "I think patients would rather step into a pleasant-smelling atmosphere than their nostrils being assaulted by a scary antiseptic hospital-like smell."

"I agree, but I don't think that's for you to decide. Next time, ask me."

"Sorry."

She wasn't sorry, but she did wonder what

bee flew up his bonnet while he was outside.

"Let the next patient know we're ready."

Courtney opened the door and waved in the next patient.

They attended to six more patients. In that time Courtney hated to, but she had to ask Blake twice for assistance with the blood-drawing procedures.

After he helped her with the last patient, he asked, "Why are you having such a difficult time? I was told you were a certified phlebotomist."

She recognized his frustration as a deep furrow formed in his brows. "I'm guessing they didn't tell you that I recently completed my phlebotomist certification, my thirty venipunctures and ten capillary punctures." Her eyes glared. She wanted to call him, Mr. Grouchy, as she did when her kids acted up, but she held that back, too.

In frustration, he shook his head, pointed to the bloody contaminated paper towels, and barked orders. "Clean this mess up." He turned and walk out of the tiny room.

She ignored his demand; instead, she demanded, "Wait just a minute. I've got a bone to pick with you."

"Excuse me, did you say you have a bone to pick with me?"

Courtney was miffed. "I don't know who you think you are, but don't think you can talk to me like that."

"Do I need to remind you that I'm your boss?" He crossed his arms in anger.

"Boss or no boss, that doesn't give you the right to talk down to me. You may need a refresher course on developing positive working relationships with staff." She held back the tears welling in her eyes. "I've dealt with far worse verbal abuse than you've dished out, but I won't tolerate even a hint of it from anyone, including you. If you have a problem with me as your assistant, tell me now, and I'll ask to be reassigned."

He decided then and there this conversation needed to end. He didn't mind the challenge; he'd been challenged by disgruntled staff before. He could fire her on the spot, but he didn't want to make a drastic decision in a heated moment. It was their first day—a stress-filled day on the job. He needed time to process, to think it through—they both needed time.

His arms relaxed to his side. His brow softened. "Let's call a truce."

Courtney's heart was beating out of her chest. She didn't want to continue the conversation, either. "It will take me a few minutes to disinfect the room, and then I'll be ready to go."

***

During the drive back to the hospital, the bus was filled with the disapproval of deafening silence. The thoughts in her head were loud. She'd allowed the rumbling emotions of her past that lie just beneath the service to erupt like a volcano. Chances were, the man sitting a few feet from her probably thought she was a raving lunatic. He might understand if she shared her turbulent past, but she wasn't ready to share her past life with this stranger. She expected the, 'don't bother showing up for work tomorrow' speech when they pulled into the parking lot. It never came.

Blake parked the bus, turned to Courtney and said, "See you in the morning." Just to remind her who was boss, he added, "Don't be late."

"See ya, tomorrow." Courtney gathered her backpack and left in a hurry.

She unlocked her car with the remote. She could hardly wait to get home, feed the kids, tuck them in bed, and take a long hot soak in her clawfoot tub. The pleasant thought lingered until she realized she had to return and start all over again in less than fifteen hours. She let out a giant sigh and started the engine.

***

By the time she arrived home, she was exhausted from the emotional and mental strain of the day and still reeling from their argument. She regretted the manner in which she delivered her thoughts; however, she didn't regret the words that needed to be said. If Blake thought he would get a call in the morning from HR informing him that she'd quit, he was mistaken. She wasn't a coward. She'd stand up to a bully and show up for another day.

***

Blake decided to grab Taco Bell and dine in his room. He wanted to be left alone.

He showered and dressed in jeans and a sweatshirt before he opened his bag of food. He'd made a special request for a microwave in his room for days like today. He was starving and ordered the $10 box with four crunchy tacos and four beefy five-layer burritos with beef, beans, sour cream, cheese, and the addictive chips and nacho cheese sauce he craved. It came with two fountain drinks. He gulped down one before he arrived at the inn. The massive meal was meant to be shared. If there was a chance he had left-overs, it would make a nice midnight snack.

He mulled over the day's events. Before the little blow-up at the end, he had been overall pleased. The clinic was cramped but well equipped. Understaffed, he'd preferred to have a Medical Assistant and a Community Health Navigator, but he wasn't in charge. It would have also been nice if both employees of the clinic weren't on medical leave simultaneously. He knew it couldn't be helped, people break bones—accidents happen, but having an experienced staff member who knew the workings of the clinic and the area would have simplified the process. Mid-day, he thought Courtney was sliding into her position comfortably. He'd thought she was more of an asset than a liability. She was even translating the local vernacular when he was stumped.

Overall, if he performed a self-evaluation performance review, he'd say, he clearly performed his job well, but there was room for improvement. Evidently, Courtney made it clear there was definitely room for improvement.

Blake decided he needed to talk to his mentor—his mom. His mother's footsteps led him to his chosen career. As a family nurse practitioner, she'd understand his staffing frustrations. She had thirty years of experience running a community care clinic in the Outer Banks.

He hadn't spoken with his parents since he arrived in Spring Valley, so most the conversation was a guided tour of the town, his accommodations, and the ins-and outs of the mobile unit. In the call, he asked his mother, "Do you think I'm too demanding?"

"That's a broad topic. I don't think you're telling me the whole story behind the question. What happened today?"

For the next few minutes, he replayed the account, word-for-word. Then, he paused, waiting for a sympathetic response. It never came.

"Honey, I'm sure you're leaving out some negative emotions that surfaced from both of you."

She was right. He'd left out several things.

"First, it's your opening day working together in a strange situation. Remember, a mobile unit has its own unique challenges in itself. Secondly, you just met this co-worker, and you have no idea of this woman's personal circumstance. You never know what goes on behind closed doors."

He felt a 'thirdly' coming. "You may be right, but—"

She finished, "Thirdly, I don't know if you've considered this, but you may be projecting your negative feelings about Karen on to your new assistant. It's a 'protect the heart mechanism.' Karen was your assistant for a long time. You worked side-by-side, day in and day out." She took a breath. "You probably don't even realize you're projecting."

He didn't reply, not even a sigh. She continued, "I've got to be honest with you, son. If things don't go the way you like, you can get testy."

"Gee, thanks Mom, that's what I love about you, you never spare the truth."

"Blake, sometimes truth hurts, but sometimes it heals."

He wasn't in the mood to talk about hurts, nor was he in the mood to talk about Karen. He tried not to even think about his ex-fiancé.

"On that note, I'll say goodbye. Need some sleep. Love you. Tell Dad hello, and I love him, too."

She knew her son well enough to know he didn't like what she had to say. But that was okay. Sometimes he needed to hear it.

"Love you, Blake." Before he had the chance to disconnect, she sneaked in a friendly reminder, "Be nice."

He threw the fancy throw pillows off the bed, thinking the name was apropos. He needed to release some tension, vent, throw something that didn't cause damage—the pillows were perfect.

He grabbed the remote from the night table and switched on the TV. He scrolled until he landed on the Surfing Live channel. He could get lost in watching the world's best surfers competing on some of the most iconic breaks in the world, sometimes in shark infested waters. There's nothing like a close encounter with a shark, he thought.

The distraction didn't keep his mind occupied. Courtney kept entering his thoughts through the cracks. He considered, maybe his mother was right—as usual. He'd never been that highly reactive in the workplace with a co-worker. He'd patiently mentored nursing assistants before. There was no viable reason for him to react that way toward Courtney. Didn't matter, he reminded himself, if he was stressed, he was going to have to apologize. He needed to wipe the slate clean. He thought they both needed a new start. Hopefully, an apology would remove any evidence of his mistake.

He texted his mom, "You're right. Thanks for your tough love."

Chapter Five

ourtney opened the door to the Mockingbird Coffee House and walked in to the smell of coffee brewing and sweet treats baking. Two of her basic food groups—coffee and sugar. She'd allowed extra time on her drive to the hospital to stop and pick up a peace offering for Blake. Sugar could tame the wildest beast. She'd hoped a slice of Ada's chess pie would do the trick for Mr. McGrumpy.

"Good morning, Courtney. I didn't expect to see you. The coffee house isn't on your way to the hospital. What brings you by so early?" Ada greeted her first customer.

"Let's just say, I don't think I made my best impression with my boss on my first day on the mobile clinic." Courtney surveyed the display of desserts behind the glass case. "I'm hoping you have chess pie available this morning."

Courtney briefed Ada on her encounter with her grumpy boss. Confused, Ada wondered if she was talking about the same man she'd met Saturday night. The man she'd thought was the ideal match for Courtney. Ada anticipated this matchmaking might be an ambitious assignment, but from what she was hearing from Courtney, it was definitely going to be challenging.

The Lord had already taken care of the toughest hurdle and placed Courtney in the mobile unit, but this battle royal was a red flag. Ada thought to herself, *I'll have my work cut out for me.*

"I've always said, a coffee a day keeps the grumpy away. Give me two of your largest black coffees and two pieces of chess pie."

Ada pulled out the pie and placed it in a pink pie box. "I'll do better than that. How about I box up a whole pie for the same price of two slices? He can nibble on it all day."

"You're an angel!" Courtney balanced the two cups on the pie box as she headed out the door. "I'll let you know how today goes. Say a little prayer for me."

"Already one step ahead of you. God bless!"

***

Courtney parked beside the bus. She was early but Blake had already arrived and the engine was running. With the addition of coffee and pie, she'd have to make two quick trips. She first grabbed her backpack, and the pie box, opened the bus door and left them on the passenger floor. She got a glimpse of Blake in the back examining room. She yelled out, "It's just me. I need to get something else from my car. I'll only be a second."

By the time she'd returned with the two coffees, Blake was getting settled into the driver's seat. He reached over to assist. "Let me help." He took the cups and placed them in the cup holders as Courtney rearranged the backpack and pie box. She hopped up in the passenger seat, ready to present her apology.

She opened the box so Blake could take a peek. She made no excuses. "I stopped at the Mockingbird Coffee House to pick up a peace offering."

He didn't look so stern this morning. The storm that brewed in his smoky, gray eyes yesterday had calmed.

"I think we were on the same wave length." He pointed to the two coffee cups on the counter.

He didn't have to apologize to Courtney. She just knew.

"You can never have too much coffee." She took a sip and smiled.

Their amicable gestures seemed to smooth their moods. Courtney knew that all was not forgotten, but it was definitely a better start to the day.

Her peace offering worked. She grinned as he pulled out of the hospital parking lot.

***

Meticulously, she prepared the examining room for the after-lunch appointments as per his instructions. From the hallway, Blake, seemingly reviewing a chart, watched her with a sense of appreciation. Her determination to succeed with the task at hand was admirable. He thought she definitely had chutzpa to speak her mind, as she so freely spoke yesterday.

"You not going to join John and me for lunch?"

There was something in the way he asked, like it was a standing invitation.

"Sure," Courtney accepted the invitation. "Give me a few seconds. I'm almost finished."

"Bring the pie, and we'll share with John."

The man wearing the blue and gold hat smiled as they approached.

"I reserved a spot for you." He knocked on the picnic table with his knuckles. "Is this the young lady I've heard so much about?"

"Depends on what you've heard." Courtney sat the pie box, lunch bag, and water bottle on the table. "I'm Courtney, the nursing assistant."

"I'm, John, the volunteer."

"Nice to meet you. Love your Buccaneer cap. You and my son would become fast friends. He's a fan of anything pirate."

"I didn't know you had a son," the revelation surprised Blake. "I thought Gracie was your only child."

"No, I'm the proud mother of two, Chance and Gracie." And Courtney thought to herself, *there's a whole lot you don't know about me.*

John sensed an underlying tension between the two, but his wife said he couldn't read emotions, so maybe he misinterpreted what type of tension they held. He thought for a second and smiled.

Blake didn't want to move on from the two-kids topic. "Chance would like my grandad's High Tider Elizabethton brogue. He adds a lot of pirate slang mixed in his speech, even though he never lived on Ocracoke, the island settled by ex-pirates."

"Last summer, Dad treated our family and a bunch of friends to a vacation in the Outer Banks. Chance was into anything and everything Blackbeard. I'm a little concerned he's going to end up on the wrong side of the law." She crossed her fingers. "Let's hope not."

"Granddad owns a bait and tackle shop; tourists find his accent charming. I think he started exaggerating his speech and hamming it up a bit for the tourists. It was good for business. They love it, especially the kids."

"I think you've done the opposite and try to conceal your accent, but you have a southern drawl with an occasional mix of old English. I've picked up on some very strong 'r's' after your vowels," Courtney teased Blake.

"I think you're imagining things."

Trying to prove a point, Courtney picked up a bag of chips, "What's in this bag?"

Blake answered without thinking, "Potater chips."

"Gotcha! You just proved my point. Yesterday, you "weeshed" for something. The long 'e' sounded a little New Zealand-ish." She grinned. A minor victory, but she won that round.

Blake crunched on his *potater* chips.

John changed the topic of conversation.

"Well, 'Proud Mother of Two,' patients have been singing your praises."

Blake raised his brows and glanced at Courtney. She ignored the look.

"I'm not the healer." She gestured toward Blake and added, "He is. I'm basically a glorified receptionist."

"No matter what you call yourself, they say you're the sweetest, kindest, most caring person they've met, and you don't make them feel ashamed."

"They have nothing to be ashamed of."

"Well, some folk find it embarrassing to have to rely on others for free health care. They're proud people and don't like to be the recipients of hand-outs."

Courtney was very familiar with shame and embarrassment, but she kept that secret to herself.

"Well, as long as I'm here, they'll always be treated with respect."

"Good to hear. Now, what's in your box?" John pointed to the pink box.

John had a sweet tooth and forgot to pack a dessert. He recognized the dessert box.

"Fresh baked chess pie from the Mockingbird Coffee House in Spring Valley," Courtney explained as she opened the box for a peek.

"Oh, I'm familiar with the Mockingbird. My sister-in-law and family live in Spring Valley. If I remember correctly, which lately it's been a hit or miss, the owner's name is…" He tapped his temple with his finger as if to loosen the name stuck somewhere in his brain. "Ada! That's the name I was searching for. She's a fine baker and the friendliest soul. We always leave with a box full of goodies."

Blake waited for John to sing his praises, but John just jammed a big bite of sugar pie in his trap.

Courtney's alarm on her phone rang, alerting them that lunch break was over. They packed up and walked back to the bus.

***

When the last patient walked out the door, Courtney saw a woman pull in the parking lot. Something told Courtney to stand in the door and wait. She sensed the young woman wearing dark sunglasses on a cloudy day needed immediate medical care. Courtney watched as the woman helped her toddler out of the old, dented car and they walked toward the bus.

Courtney got Blake's attention and mouthed, "One more."

He looked at his watch and then nodded to give her the go-ahead.

"You made it just in time." Courtney greeted the two and helped the toddler up the steps.

"Just have a seat, and we'll get you registered."

The woman never removed her shades.

Courtney finished the patient intake and asked, "How can we help you?"

The patient lifted her hand to the sunglasses and removed them revealing a black eye and a bloody band aide covering an open wound.

"I think I'm going to need a few stitches," she meekly replied.

"It sure looks that way. What happened?"

Courtney knew what happened, and she also knew truth would not cross her patient's lips. Truth had a way of making matters worse.

"I was carrying a basket full of dirty laundry, tripped on one of her toys, and fell down the steps."

"Well, don't you worry, sweetheart. We'll fix you up in no time."

Blake walked down the narrow hallway to escort his patient to an examining room. Courtney reached for the toddler's hand. "I have a fun coloring book. Would you like to stay with me and color?" She picked up a baggie. "I have a bag of Cheerios we can snack on."

The little girl held a tight grip on her mother's jeans.

Assuring her, she squeezed her tight and put her daughter's hand into Courtney's. "You'll be alright. This nice lady will keep you company while momma gets fixed up."

It took longer than Courtney expected. At the slightest noise or hearing the sound of her mother's voice, the little girl kept glancing to see when her mother would return. She was relieved when her mom and Blake walked back down the hallway.

The woman zipped her child's coat and in slow motion pulled her coat over her bruised shoulder. Courtney stuffed a piece of paper in the woman's pocket. "Sweetie, if you ever fall down the steps again and you need help, you can call me day or night, and I'll take you to the doctor."

Tears welled in the woman's eyes. She knew Courtney was talking in code. Abused women have a sixth sense when it comes to other victims. She reached for Courtney's hand and gave her a gentle squeeze.

On the drive back to the hospital, Blake discussed their last patient with Courtney.

"That was kind of you to offer after hours assistance," Blake glanced over to Courtney, who sat quietly. "I suspect there may be domestic abuse; however, her injuries were consistent with the fall that she described. But if she returns with similar injuries, I'm obligated to report."

"In the intake, I asked if she felt safe at home, and she said she did."

Courtney wasn't willing to tell her story, and she didn't want to go into the debated discussion of why women stay in an abusive situation. She also didn't want to reveal secrets of her past she kept hidden in a corner of her heart.

"I just wanted her to know she had a lifeline she could grab. I'll follow-up with her next week to make sure she returns to have her stitches removed."

"I like how you immediately develop a genuine connection with patients. I'll be the first to admit I lack in that area. After two years in the midst of working with COVID patients, I built a barrier between my patients and me. Because of the emotional toll and the constant trauma of death, for self-preservation, I tended to physical needs and let nurses tend to the emotional distress of patients." He paused for a moment, "But walking through the fire, I was forced to learn the importance of psychological needs, to listen to what's going on in a patient's life."

"I've found that no matter your walk of life, it's important to express empathy." Her eyes misted over. "I try."

"The one thing that puzzles me is why these people don't move to find jobs and better health care."

The atmosphere in the bus immediately fell from warm to freezing.

"*These people*, as you call them, are self-reliant. They love their mountain community, they love their people, their churches, and they cling to their faith. It's their lifeline. Their communities may be economically deprived, but their shared history keeps them glued to their community."

The words were on the tip of his tongue, *you might want to knock that chip off your shoulder,* but he held them back. He didn't want a repeat of yesterday, so instead he shared a piece of his family tree.

"I'm sorry. I didn't mean to offend with my comment. I understand what you're conveying. The Foster's, my mother's side of the family, have lived on the Outer Banks since the 1700s. We can trace our ancestry back to the shipwrecked English, Scottish-Irish immigrants, seeking a better life in the colonies."

He looked over and saw that Courtney's fire had smoldered. He continued with his story. "For centuries, they were isolated on the island, much like your Scottish-Irish immigrants were isolated in Appalachia. Water isolated my people, mountains isolated yours."

Blake gave her a brief history of how before World War II, villagers lived on the remote island and fished. After the war, bridges were built that linked the island to the mainland. In the last few decades, developers swallowed up the island and covered the beaches with hundreds of stilted condo rentals.

"Our descendants were, and still are, seafaring folk. Fishing has been the mainstay of the Outer Banks for centuries. Hurricanes belting the island with ferocious winds tried to drive my ancestors off the island, but they'd survived and would rebuild time and time again. They were strong like the majestic Southern oak. Their roots run deep."

"That's exactly my point," Courtney explained. "Appalachian mountain roots run deep."

"I guess I could ask the same question of my people. Why didn't they move to the mainland? Life would have been easier, but it's their home. Their souls are connected to the sandy soil."

"Next time, I'll share my family connections to these mountains." She winked at him. "Some of the stories, you won't believe."

As Blake pulled into the hospital parking lot, he wondered what to do about the woman who sat in the passenger seat. She drove him crazy—but in a good way.

They parted ways with Courtney getting in her car and Blake walking across the parking lot to the hospital to check in with the main office.

He'd lost sleep the night before, worrying over how to apologize to Courtney for his rude behavior. Tonight, he'd lose sleep worrying if she'd show up the following morning.

Chapter Six

Saturday morning, Courtney rolled over to tap off the alarm clock on her smartphone. She'd set it on an extra loud ringtone because she knew she would have a hard time rolling out of the bed. She lay dazed and confused, until she heard the songbirds chirping their morning chorus. The birds had survived the night challenges and announced they were ready to face a new day.

She could identify with her feathered friends. She accepted the temporary Health Bus assignment because it was only three days a week, and since it fell during the holidays, the short work week would give her more time with the kids during Christmas. The first three days were challenging—to say the least. She congratulated herself on surviving.

Lazily, she stayed in bed, and her mind drifted to Blake. She'd never worked in such cramped quarters. Hospital rooms were small, but nothing compared to the mobile unit. It wasn't so much the confined space; the real dilemma was working alongside Blake so closely. If he'd been old enough to be her father, she wouldn't have thought twice about it. But he wasn't. Blake was young, attractive, and as far as she knew—single. At times, that combination was a little unsettling. Three months in a mobile unit could be a very long time, especially since she was insecure in her position as a nursing assistant, and although he said nothing, she could sense he was disappointed that he wasn't provided a medical assistant. She'd have to make it work—her career depended on it.

She knew her body wouldn't wake by itself, and she needed coffee. She threw back the covers, grabbed her cozy housecoat and slippers, and then stumbled to the kitchen and the coffee maker. The kids were still sound asleep. Gracie's cat Angel zigzagged down the hallway, yawning and stretching along the way. She rubbed against Courtney's ankles and, looking upward, purred a hello. Courtney reciprocated, bent down, and scratched the cat's head. A soft feline-contented purr followed.

Courtney called this time suspension *perkatory*: the miserable, drawn-out period waiting for fresh coffee to brew. After the final drip, she poured the strong black coffee in a mug, added one teaspoon of sugar and two splashes of cream, stirred, and took her first sip standing at the window, watching the colorful leaves flutter to the ground.

At first glance, it appeared the weather would cooperate for their mountain hike at Gabe and Shauna's cabin at the lake. The kids had been looking forward to the outdoor adventure. Over the last two years, Courtney felt adopted by her father's best friend, Ryan, and his family. They welcomed Courtney and her children with open arms. Ryan's daughters, Shauna and Abby, added Courtney to their best friend category, making her feel as if she'd gained sisters.

Gabe and Tyler, Abby's husband, would serve as guides for the hike. Gabe's outdoor adventure tour company had grown into a thriving business specializing in trail hiking, fly fishing in the river, water rafting, kayaking on the lake, and winter backcountry skiing. Today, Chance and Gracie would hit the trail with their friends, Bryce and Paige, and kids from their church youth group while the women would hang around the cabin and just take a break from the stress of daily life. She looked forward to some girl talk with her friends.

The caffeine provided the jolt she needed to shower and dress for the day. But first, the unmade bed needed tending to. She required an orderly and balanced home because it calmed her. She felt the little things in life mattered. Coffee and making the bed each morning started her day off right.

For today's activities, layering would be required. Just in case her relaxing in the cabin plans were derailed, hiking attire was a must. From the closet, she pulled out a long sleeve shirt, trail running leggings, hiking shoes, and a rain jacket in case the weather turned for the worst. She'd throw in a heavier fleece jacket for the evening's cooler weather around the campfire and a warm, comfy beanie.

"Mom!"

Courtney's quiet time ended.

"Chance, don't yell. You'll wake your sister." This was one of the few mornings that Courtney didn't wake up with Gracie cuddled up against her in bed. Her daughter's nightmares robbed them both of peaceful sleep. Courtney pulled her hair up into a pony tail and began her mom duties.

"I'm hungry. What's for breakfast?"

Chance was always hungry. "Remember, it's Saturday, and we're having a big breakfast at Papaw Rich and Nana Alana's."

"But I'm hungry now."

"You can have a Pop Tart if you don't report me to the food police. It's not the most nutritious food source, but we'll consider it a breakfast appetizer." She walked into Chance's room to find him cuddling the corgi. Her patience was growing thin, but that scene melted her heart.

"Can Nick go with us?"

The pup lifted his head and gave Courtney a side-eyed glance as if waiting to hear the answer.

"No, he's staying at your grandfather's. He's not the best trail dog. He tends to wander off, and we don't want him to get lost in the woods."

Chance gave his mom the feel sorry for me pout. "Would you get me a Pop Tart? I can have breakfast in bed." Chance pulled the covers up around his chin.

"If you're starving, you can mosey in the kitchen and get your own Pop Tart." Courtney started gathering clothes he needed for the hike and laid them at the foot of his bed.

"Mom!"

She glared at Chance. "You woke your sister." She leaned down and kissed his forehead.

"I'll be right there, Gracie."

Before she got to Gracie's room, someone rang the doorbell.

"Gracie, it's time to get out of bed. I've got to see who's at the door."

She opened the door. "Dad, what are you doing here? I thought you were cooking us breakfast."

"Alana's cooking. I just thought I'd pop over and see if you needed help getting the kids moving this morning."

She hugged and kissed him on the cheek. "You're a life saver. I just pulled together Chance's hiking clothes. If you get him on the move, I'll get Gracie started." Without Rich asking, she went straight for the coffee maker and poured him a cup.

"You know me well, daughter."

"Where there is coffee, there is happiness."

***

Courtney enjoyed visiting Gabe and Shauna, what she didn't enjoy was the treacherous drive to the mountain cabin. She would love to relish what was left of the gorgeous colorful fall foliage, but she had to keep her eyes on the road that snaked high in the hills. With its crazy twists and hairpin turns through forested areas, she was in constant prayer that she wouldn't meet an oncoming vehicle on the narrow lane and leave the pavement to be swallowed up by the forest with bits and pieces of their car left dangling in the branches of the trees. The kids thought it was fun and thrilling as if they were riding a roller coaster. Courtney found the adrenaline-fueled adventure to be terrifying.

High on top of the mountain at the end of the paved road, a river rock driveway led to the cabin and Gabe's outdoor adventure touring company. Though jarring, Courtney thought the organic river rock gave the driveway a natural and almost rustic look. She loosened her tight grip on the steering wheel and puffed out a sigh of relief. Courtney pulled up near the cabin and parked the car beside the storage shed. Wall mounted racks attached to the shed held a rainbow of colorful kayaks.

"I want the turquoise kayak!" Gracie yelled out her selection.

"I'll take the orange one."

"Nobody is taking a kayak," Courtney reminded the kids. "Today's outdoor adventure is hiking."

"But—"

"No buts about it. Don't even mention kayaks." She looked in the rear-view mirror to make eye contact. "Do you understand?"

Gracie and Chance nodded their heads.

"I need a verbal response."

"Yes, ma'am, we understand," they chimed in chorus.

Courtney smiled pridefully. It always pleased her when her children remembered manners, even though presented begrudgingly.

"Looks like we're the first to arrive."

Before Courtney could unbuckle her seatbelt, the passengers in the back seat were already out of the car and running toward the cabin. Shauna and Gabe stepped out on the porch to greet their guests. You could hear their chocolate lab's excited yip-yipping before he appeared out of nowhere from the woods and made a beeline for Chance who immediately grabbed a stick and started playing fetch. Gracie followed close behind.

The crisp fall air was invigorating and held a sweet scent of pine sap. When Courtney stepped out of the car and inhaled a deep breath then exhaled, she felt stress escaping from her body. She could hear the tap-tap-tap of a woodpecker pecking away at a tree in search of a meal of ants or spiders hiding underneath the bark. A light breeze rustled the leaves, and in the distance, the soothing sound of a trickling stream meant a creek was nearby. Today would be her escape into nature with friends. A time to share her deepest thoughts, feelings, and frustrations of the past week.

Shauna walked out to greet Courtney.

How does she always look so stunning, Courtney thought. *Maybe, it's because she doesn't have children to chase around.* Shauna was trim and fit. A testament to an active outdoor lifestyle. Her fiery, curly red mane matched her outgoing and vibrant personality. She held a strong, courageous spirit that carried her through a traumatic past and eventually enabled her to open her heart to love again when she met Gabe in Spring Valley. She was an inspiration. Their friendship was a blessing.

"Do you need any help?"

Courtney reached in the back to retrieve the kids backpacks. "I would love some help; the kids ran off without their gear."

Before she took the backpacks, Shauna hugged Courtney. "I'm so glad you're here. It's been too long between our friendship breaks."

"I know, I've been crazy busy, but I've been looking forward to today. Even if it's just a few hours while the kids are hiking, I'll take it."

"Abby just called, and they're running a few minutes late, as usual. They're leading the caravan, so get ready for mayhem when they arrive. It's a small group. I think with yours and Abby's twins, there will be a total of ten kids. But once we get everyone out on the trail, I promise a relaxing afternoon."

"I'm going to hold you to it."

From a distance the crunching sound of car wheels rolling on gravel was an indication that the caravan had made up for lost time, and in a matter of moments mayhem would commence.

The kids and dog ran around the cabin to the porch where Shauna and Courtney lined up the backpacks as three vehicles came into view. Abby and her family were in the lead car, followed by a small passenger van driven by the youth pastor, then a red jeep, similar to what Blake drove.

There's no way Blake would be part of the caravan, was all Courtney could think. Right up until the jeep's door opened, and Blake stepped out.

She didn't mean to, but she said it out loud, "For heaven's sake, what in the world is he doing here?"

"Sounds like you know him," Shauna sounded surprised.

"You could say that." With raised eyebrows Courtney looked at Shauna. "I haven't had time to fill you in on my new nursing position. We've got a lot to catch up on."

"Gabe met him this week when Gabe was visiting his mom at the inn and invited Blake to join the hike," Shauna explained.

"Lovely," Courtney quipped.

***

As lovely as he was the first time they met at Spring Valley Inn, Courtney decided. She eyed him secretly from behind her dark, polarized sunglasses. She felt a sudden ridiculous sense of butterflies fluttering around in her stomach. She liked this laid-backed version of Blake as opposed to rigid work-Blake. His messy sun-bleached hair had an adventure-ready appeal. From the looks of his attire, she guessed that he'd dropped a wad of cash at the local outdoor sporting store. He'd layered with a long sleeve shirt and underneath a next-to-skin compression tee that accentuated his muscular physique. His grey fleece cargo pants matched his smoky grey eyes. The mid-ankle hiking boots were a perfect choice for the ensemble.

As he walked toward the cabin, he was just as surprised to see her. "Courtney, I didn't expect to see you here."

"I'm just as surprised as you are. Are you a stalker?" she teased. "I'm trying to decide if I should be concerned."

"I swear, I had no idea. I met Gabe at the inn, and he invited me to join the hike."

Shauna extended her hand to Blake. "I'm Shauna. Gabe is my husband. Welcome!"

"Nice to meet you." Blake took in the scenery. "This is gorgeous! I've lived my whole life on the coast, but I could get use to this isolation. The higher we drove, I left all the worries of the world in the valley."

"I call it Peaceful Cabin. Living here has a way of calming my soul." Shauna took a deep breath. "I wasn't sold on the isolation in the beginning, but now, I can't imagine living anywhere else."

Gabe blew his whistle to gather the group.

"Let's get our backpacks on and head out. Does everyone have their emergency whistle?"

An ear-piercing screech of whistles confirmed.

"I'm going to give you a quiz. Answer with your whistles," Gabe instructed.

"What is the signal for 'Help me'?"

Three blasts of the high-pitched whistles erupted.

"Correct. Now, what is a call-back signal which means, 'Come here'?"

The group let out two blasts.

"Excellent. What blast means, 'Where are you'?"

One loud blast of "FWEET!" followed.

Gabe proceeded to go over hiking etiquette with the junior hikers and introduced Tyler and Blake as the guides.

"Grab your gear, find a partner, and we'll start this hiking adventure."

"I'm now on duty, so we'll talk afterwards," Blake promised Courtney and Shauna.

Courtney just smiled at Blake as she helped her kids with their backpacks and reminded them to do exactly what they were told.

Courtney, Shauna, and Abby waved goodbye to the hikers. Still smiling and waving, Courtney murmured, "Alright. By my calculations, we have about three kid-free hours." Courtney was as giddy as a teen who had friends over to hang out. They turned and danced their way inside the cabin.

Chapter Seven

Courtney had so much to share about her recent life developments. She wanted advice about Blake who'd shown up unexpectedly and was getting and up close and personal insight into her parenting skills on the hike with her children. She hoped the kids were on their best behavior. Courtney worried as she stepped into the cabin. She needed to talk with her friends about her work situation and how she should handle it. How to manage the single-mom title. How to help Gracie heal her emotional scars that had recently surfaced in her recurring nightmares.

Courtney felt as if she were still walking in the wonder of the forest as she stepped into the entryway, walls adorned with beautiful birch tree wallpaper that evoked instant tranquility. The first time she stood here two years prior, Courtney was hesitant to enter. Shauna and Abby had opened their hearts to a wounded woman hoping to help Courtney heal. But she was reluctant to leave her children—even for just a few hours. Reluctant to open up to others, suspicious of their motives and fearful of judgement. Reluctant to trust because of the hurt experienced from people in her past that had broken her trust.

How different she was from the woman who stood there two years ago. Courtney was so thankful that she didn't deny Shauna and Abby the opportunity to walk beside her in her healing journey. Their friendship was the connection, support, and encouragement she needed to begin the healing process. Courtney was convinced that God had placed these two godly women in her life at that specific moment in time. She couldn't imagine life without them. Sometimes she'd pinch herself just to make sure she wasn't dreaming.

"Who wants coffee?" Shauna led the way to the kitchen.

"That's a silly question. All I want is coffee." Courtney was surprised she even asked.

"Decaf?"

"Decaf? If you drink decaf, you might as well just drink hot water."

"I know. Just thought you might want a more calming beverage."

Abby opened the cabinet door to retrieve the mugs. "If you've got cocoa, I'll take a hot cocoa."

"I picked up your favorite double chocolate cocoa this week. It's in the cabinet to your right." Shauna knew that her sister's first choice would always be hot-chocolate topped with whipped-cream. "You're going to love it; it has bits of real dark chocolate blended with the cocoa."

Abby found the cocoa and did a happy dance.

"You're the only person I know that drinks hot-cocoa all year long." Courtney reserved hot chocolate for holidays.

"You're the only person I know that would prefer an IV drip of coffee over a coffee mug."

Courtney laughed.

"Once I switched from coffee to cocoa, I'll never go back."

"That's blasphemous!" Courtney jeered.

"Seriously, coffee makes me jittery and cranky. Once I gave it up and switched to hot chocolate, I started sleeping like a baby," Abby defended her beverage choice.

"More power to you. I'm not responsible for my actions without my coffee."

Courtney pulled out the bar stool and made herself comfortable. The kitchen was rustic and cozy with log walls, custom bubble glass-fronted wood cabinetry, exposed wood beams, and earth toned granite countertops. It opened into the great room featuring a wood burning fireplace with a floor to ceiling natural stone hearth. The scent of the coffee blended with the smell of cocoa shared with friends triggered feelings of happiness. Courtney felt having coffee with friends was the best therapy.

"Let's take our drinks and move to the family room." Shauna held a plate of brownies as she walked over and placed them on the coffee table.

"I didn't know you made brownies. They look delicious." Abby had never met a brownie she didn't like.

***

Shauna cocked a questioning eyebrow. "Okay, Courtney, you said we have a lot of catching up to do. How do you know Mr. McDreamy? Gabe said he was in town working with the Health Bus. Did you meet him at the hospital?"

Courtney rolled her eyes. "Not only did I meet him, I've been assigned to work on the Health Bus—with him."

Abby's bright smile and wide eyes revealed her approval. "Really? What's he like?"

"He may resemble Mr. McDreamy, but my nickname for him is Mr. McGrumpy. He's one of the things I wanted to talk about and get your opinions on how to proceed."

"I'd proceed full steam ahead," Abby blurted out.

Shauna could sense that Courtney had serious concerns. "We're just teasing you. You said you had a lot to catch up on, tell us what's going on."

Courtney spent the next few minutes telling them how she ended up on the mobile unit. Describing her experiences, her insecurities, and Blake's grumpy demeanor, she relayed her fear of being fired and her peace-offering gesture.

"I hear what you're saying, but maybe it's just adjusting to new circumstances. Gabe has chatted with him a few times at the inn, and his first impression of Blake was positive. He said he was friendly, easy going, and personable. He was impressed that when he invited him to join the hike, Blake said he'd been a youth group leader at his church in the Outer Banks."

"That's interesting. I don't know a lot about his background. It's mainly been strictly business this past week."

Abby added with a nod, "We chatted a few minutes about his traveling medical assignment before we drove out this morning. I was fascinated."

"Maybe you have your guard up because he's an attractive, young, single man," Shauna suggested.

"Hey, I'm not on the hunt for a husband. I just want to keep my job." Courtney was well aware of the unsettling fact that Blake was an attractive, young, single man.

"Then I wouldn't worry about it. Just be you, do your job, and take one day at a time." Abby took a bite of her brownie. "He'll come around. Everybody loves you."

"Thank you! That was a kind thing to say." Those words warmed Courtney's heart. "Enough about me. Abby, I hear you're the director of the Christmas play at the theater this year."

"Yes, I'm insane. This is the busiest time of the year at the store, and I agreed to direct."

"Mom knows how much you love the theatre. I'm sure she'll understand." It amazed Shauna how well her sister and mother managed to maintain a happy, healthy, mother-daughter relationship at the Old Towne Christmas Shop her mother owned and Abby co-managed. When Shauna graduated high school and went to college, all she wanted to do was escape her 24/7 Christmas life of her mother's business. It was fun as a child but grew tiring year-after-year for Shauna, but Abby followed in her mother's Christmas-themed footsteps. The thought of ever wanting to escape Spring Valley seemed foreign now to Shauna. Returning and reconnecting to her family roots was exactly what she needed to move forward in her life. Plus, if she hadn't returned, she'd never met Gabe, the love of her life.

"There will definitely be time management involved, but I think I can do it with a little help from my friends."

"Don't look at me. I'm not an actress," Courtney raised her hand in protest.

"I wasn't thinking of you, but I had Gracie in mind for a supporting role." Privately, Abby thought it would be good for Gracie to mingle with other children. She continued with her sales pitch. "The play is based on Gloria Houston's children's book, *The Year of the Perfect Christmas Tree*. It's an incredible Appalachian story. I was introduced to it when someone gave it to the twins as a present."

"You can ask her, but I don't think you'll get the response you're looking for. She really enjoys playing with Paige, but I don't know if a role in a play would stress her out."

"She might surprise you. It may be just what she needs."

"Since we're talking about Gracie, I wanted to ask your opinion on something."

Courtney shared how Gracie had been having a recurring nightmare and ended up in her bed several nights a week, but when she asked her to describe the dream, she says she doesn't want to because it's too scary.

"Have you talked to a therapist about it?" Abby inquired.

"No, I thought if I could get her to open up to me, we could get beyond the nightmare."

"A woman in our church delt with domestic violence when her children were very young." Abby knew this was a sensitive subject, but they were always open and honest with each other about their past. "Her youngest daughter had a recurring nightmare, and when she shared the dream, detail by detail with her, the mother realized it wasn't just a dream but a real traumatic incident of their past. When she confirmed that it was an actual event, and when the daughter learned the truth, the nightmares ended."

"So, you think something buried deep in Gracie's subconscious level is surfacing? She was so young; I had hoped she didn't remember." She wanted to believe that she'd shielded her children, but deep down, she knew the abuse, even though directed at her, would have lasting effects on her children.

"It might be. When my kids have nightmares, I ask a lot of questions and try to talk them through their dreams. It always seems to help when we bring dark thoughts out it out into the light."

The thought that her daughter might be reliving terror in her dreams broke Courtney's heart. Her eyes misted over as she blinked back the tears.

Their afternoon girl break ended up being time well spent with friends. The conversations bounced from one topic to another as they talked, laughed, cried, and ate their way through dessert, popcorn, and several beverage refills. Shauna received a text from Gabe alerting her that the hikers were on their way back to the cabin. "Sorry girls, but all good things must come to an end."

***

When the church van, filled with weary hikers, drove down the gravel lane, the men joined the women for a little relaxation on the porch while the kids gathered wood for the firepit. Shauna brought out a bucket filled with water bottles.

"How did it go?" Shauna handed Gabe a bottle.

"It was great. No one got lost, bit, or broke anything."

"I would call it a great success," Tyler, Abby's husband, agreed.

"I thought they were a great bunch of kids and well-behaved," Blake praised the youth group.

As the sun dipped below the mountains, the air cooled. Gabe announced he'd get the tinder to add to what the kids had gathered for the firepit.

"Blake, you're welcome to stay and join us for a wiener roast and smores," Shauna said.

Courtney shot Shauna a curious look wondering if Shauna and Gabe were up to clandestine matchmaking. In response, Shauna shrugged her shoulders.

"Lovely." Courtney murmured under her breath.

"I don't have anywhere to run off to. A campfire sounds great!" Blake caught a glimpse of Courtney's panicked eyes. It humored him. As he stood to join Gabe at the firepit, Blake smiled at Courtney.

He imagined her sitting close beside him, snuggled up in a blanket on the log bench under the full Harvest Moon on this night so clear they could gaze upon millions of brilliant stars.

Frustrated with the trajectory of his thoughts, Blake set his sights on the task at hand as he gathered an armful of wood. He surprised himself that he felt a connection with Courtney— he found her intriguing. He'd emotionally closed his heart for so long, it had numbed. He'd hardly noticed his cold heart had warmed.

The kids lost interest in gathering wood when Gabe and Blake starting arranging the logs and tender. When fireflies emerged from the floor of the forest, the kids and dog started chasing the flickering, tiny yellow lights that they were convinced were fairies dancing through the night.

"Don't get out of our sight," Courtney yelled. "No venturing beyond the edge of the trees." The fun-filled woods they'd just hiked in earlier that day took on dark, sinister feel as leaves rustling on the ground sounded like footsteps, and branches blowing in the wind created mysterious shadows. She went into Mom Mode and decided to break from the adults and join the kids chasing the dancing fairies in the woods. Once or twice, she glanced back toward the cabin to see how the fire was coming along. She'd hardly thought about her boss who watched and waited for her return.

***

They'd devoured the hot dogs and had moved on to roasting marshmallows. Shauna leaned over and whispered in her husband's ear, "Do you see what I see?"

Gabe looked around the campfire puzzled. "What am I supposed to be seeing?"

"Sparks flying."

"Where?" Gabe panicked. "Do I need to stomp them out?"

Shauna laughed at her clueless husband. "No, sparks flying between Courtney and Blake."

He watched them for a few seconds and suddenly became aware of the chemistry between Courtney and Blake. It reminded him of how sparks flew when he and Shauna first sat around a campfire. The night their lips first met. The night he knew he was in love with Shauna. He leaned in and kissed his wife. "I love a good campfire romance."

"It makes a great beginning to a love story." Shauna had prayed her friend would find love again. Shauna knew all about Divine appointments with love. She wondered if Courtney and Blake realized they were on a Divine date. She smiled at the thought.

Chapter Eight

The burning pain in her chest was so common that Ada ignored it, contributing the discomfort to consuming too much coffee. Afterall, her Mockingbird Coffee House was voted the best coffee shop five years in a row in Spring Valley. What would customers think if she quit drinking her own coffee? When the pain worsened, the thought occurred that she could switch to decaffeinated, but if she did, she would miss the caffeine boost that got her through until closing. She kept a roll of Tums in her apron pocket for fast relief. She popped one in her mouth, chewed vigorously, swallowed, and went about closing up the shop. She locked the door and turned the sign over that read, Closed. She had a crew in the kitchen cleaning coffee pots, dishes, and equipment. Her crew was carefully cleaning the counters, wiping out the refrigerator, and sweeping and mopping the entire area. One employee was in the balcony, cleaning tables and putting up chairs, while Ada concentrated on overseeing the downstairs cleanup and counting out the cash drawer.

Now, at sixty-one, not only did Ada notice more wrinkles and her waistline expanding, but she also knew the extreme fatigue she experienced was annoying. Still, she tried not to complain because her business had survived the shutdown when others weren't so fortunate. After retiring from teaching and pursuing her dream of opening a coffee house, she became a success story in Spring Valley's downtown business community. She wouldn't call it an over-night success, but she'd made it past the critical three-year mark and was showing a profit when the pandemic brought the world and her business to a screeching halt. During those dark, stressful days, she feared the coffee house would fail. Statistically, even without the shutdown, the business was still in the survival stage, which made the pandemic years dangerous years for any business. But miraculously, the business pulled through, and she continued with what she considered her divine calling, to minister and bless all who entered the doors. *You will be blessed when you come in and blessed when you go out* was the scripture she lived by. She'd always been a woman of prayer, but it took on a new dimension during those fearful times. Her faith in God's word and powerful prayer carried her through, drawing her even closer to God than ever before in her lifetime.

Her husband, J.R., was always worrying and suggesting that she delegate responsibilities, even to go as far as saying she needed to let go of one or more of her pet projects. Ada locked the door and took a seat at a table to catch her breath and give her time to think. She was glad it was Saturday night; she welcomed the Sunday break.

It was easy for J.R. to say, but how could she choose to let go of any of her *pet projects*? Her *pet projects* were more than just a task she did in her spare time. They were meaningful ministries. How could she choose to let go of any one of them? She'd admit she could try harder training or hiring a baker. She was known for her divine desserts, but surely, she could find someone to follow her recipes. The annual Giving Tree project she sponsored at Christmas had inspired a movement of generosity in Spring Valley and brought so much hope and joy to needy families during the holidays. Surely, she thought, J.R. didn't expect her to give that up. And she couldn't imagine not volunteering at Haven House; after all, she spearheaded the ministry for the women's rescue shelter that provided a safe house for women and children who were victims of domestic violence. She also claimed the title, First Lady, at the AME Zion Church. She was certain, J.R. wanted her to continue working side-by-side with him at church.

Now, she'd admit that her matchmaking was a *pet project*. But it really didn't require a lot of additional work. Connecting people was basically all about timing and praying. That made her wonder if the chess pie peace offering had worked for Courtney. She hadn't heard anything, but Ada wasn't worried. If those two young ones were meant to be together, it would happen. She just got a kick out of being part of the process.

As she contemplated her overcommitted calendar, she broke out in a cold sweat. She starting fanning her face with her hand and then wiped her forehead with napkins left at the table. She decided she'd think about delegating in the new year. She also decided she was going to do something she hadn't done in years. She was exhausted and when Sunday rolled around, she was going to sleep in on that morning. Without her at church, maybe J.R. would be singing a different tune about her *pet projects*.

Chapter Nine

The moment she opened the passenger door, looked at him and smiled, Blake's heart leaped. At the campfire Saturday night, they laughed, teased, and even flirted. In a crowd of ten, he felt they shared intimacy. He'd sensed any animosity between them from the previous work week burn down to embers like the burning logs. That evening, after they'd gone their separate ways, she'd left him frustrated and unsettled. All he could think of on Sunday was Courtney. Daily, his fondness for her grew. It made him want to abandon his policy of never dating a co-worker and reconsider matters of love. He considered that Courtney may just be the woman for him.

"Good morning!" Courtney greeted him. "It's a great day for ducks." She unzipped her rain jacket and draped it on the back of her seat to let it dry.

Her scent filled the air. An aromatic bouquet of magnolia enraptured his senses. Light, feminine, and intoxicating. A blend of captivating sweet and slightly spicy fragrance—the scent of romance. It reminded him of the Southern Magnolia tree in his grandmother's yard where on a hot day, he would lounge in the shade—a balm of coziness. It was one of the first things he noticed about Courtney when they first met. He remembered when she delivered coffee to his hotel room, how her scent lingered after she left.

"I just looked at the weather app, and rain is forecasted for the entire day." Blake couldn't believe they started their conversation on the topic of weather.

"From what I've heard, the rain won't keep the patients away."

Courtney dug a scrunchie out of her purse and pulled her hair up in a ponytail. Blake thought it gave her a young and fresh look that matched her fragrance. She turned and looked at Blake and smiled. Her whispery, feathered bangs added softness framing her enchanting, golden brown eyes that reflected contentment. *Today is a new beginning*, he thought to himself. *An undeserved and unexpected gift.* Blake cast his eyes to the road.

***

Their destination was less than twenty miles out of town, but it took almost forty-five minutes driving the narrow, winding roads that led to a little white country church, tucked back in a hollow, encircled by mountains. A kaleidoscope of fall colors swirled in the air as the wind and rain knocked off the amber, red, and russet leaves.

"They warned me we would be off the beaten path today, but I didn't expect to be out in the middle of nowhere," Blake bemoaned.

He also didn't expect to see two Catholic

nuns dressed in white Indian sarees, draped in
Bengali style with three blue strips and a matching
headscarf, getting out of a late model Toyota
Land Cruiser. "If I didn't know better, I would say
Mother Teresa just stepped out of that SUV."

As Blake pulled in the tiny parking lot,
Courtney happily filled him in on the volunteers.

"About forty years ago, Mother Teresa came
from Calcutta and opened the Missionaries of
Charity in Appalachia. It was the first rural
mission she opened in America. If I remember
correctly, four nuns live in the convent. As you
can tell by looking, the Sisters are originally
from India and are known around the mountains
for serving the poorest of the poor. They spend
their days visiting the poor, sick, and elderly.
They'll do whatever is needed. Wash clothes,
mow grass, provide food, pray, talk, and provide
transportation to doctors' visits, and evidently,
they also volunteer for the Health Bus." She smiled
and waved at the nuns as they popped up their
umbrellas and stood in the rain, ready to assist.

"You've got to admit, it's a surprising sight."

"Oh, it is surprising, all right, but it's also an
inspiring, beautiful sight." Courtney made her way
to the side door of the bus to greet the nuns. Before
she opened the door, she turned to Blake and said,
"I think God showed up today."

***

By the time they finished with their last patient,
even though the rain had stopped, the gravel

parking lot had almost turned to a pool of mud from the Sunday evening torrential rainfall and the steady rain all throughout the day. With the weight of the heavy bus, the tires dug deep. It concerned Blake that he'd misjudged the lot's condition. As he backed up in the soft gravel, the rear tires slid off the ledge on the side of the mountain. Blake knew getting out of the mud would be tricky. He tried to maneuver out, turning the steering wheel left, then right, shifting in reverse then quickly shifting forward attempting to rock out of the mud, but the tires held out against his useless attempts. He jumped out to inspect. In a matter of seconds, he was ankle-deep in slimy mud. He held on to the back bumper and leaned over for a closer look. He stood glaring at the tires, sunk deep in the mire, buried to the axle.

"That doesn't look good," Courtney commented. She was on the opposite side surveying the situation. Watching Blake glare at the muck and mire amused her. She had a bad habit of finding humor in exasperating circumstances, but she managed to conceal her amusement.

He didn't know she had been standing there. "You didn't have to get out in the mud. I have things under control," Blake tried to convince himself.

"You could have fooled me," she said, staring at the stuck vehicle, biting her lips to hold back the grin that was forming.

He hated to admit defeat. Annoyed with himself for backing the bus off the ledge and embarrassed that he would be forced to call a tow truck to get them out of the predicament, he looked like a volcano ready to blow. As he stomped his shoes caked with mud, from the corner of his eye he caught a glimpse of the Sisters walking toward the bus, adding to the uninvited audience.

Blake was determined to rectify the situation and climbed back in the driver's seat for one more try. He shifted in gear and pushed the gas. He'd wished the Sisters hadn't stood so close, as mud rained down on their white linen, blue bordered saris.

Blake immediately stopped and jumped out of the bus to begin his apology tour. He expected to be reprimanded by incensed nuns; instead, they laughed hysterically. For a moment, Blake stood frozen watching as the women began flinging mud at each other. He couldn't believe his eyes; he expected at any moment for the display to turn into full blown mud wrestling. He shook his head in amazement. Courtney joined him as they watched. Blake's mood transformed as a grin tugged at his mouth. Courtney doubled over laughing.

As quickly as it started, it stopped. "Well, that was fun." Sister Divya exclaimed in her sing-song cadence. She removed her glasses and began wiping them with the hem of her sari. It proved to be a futile attempt.

"I am so sorry." Blake reached out to guide them out of the mud. "Are you okay?"

"That was the most fun I've had in ages." Sister Prisha turned and pointed to the axles buried in the mud. "I'm just sorry you're stuck."

"You and me both," Blake muttered.

"We were pulling out of the lot when we saw your predicament. We don't have cell phones, but I flagged down your last patient and asked him to call a local towing company. They called, but the tow truck can't get here until tomorrow morning." She handed him a slip of paper with the towing company's number and studied his face for a reaction. "So, I guess you're stuck here until morning." Sister Prisha grinned at her own joke.

Blake crossed his arms and stared at the bus. "Looks like we have no other choice."

Sister Divya offered, "We have room in the SUV. You're welcome to ride back down the mountain with us."

Courtney suggested, "Thank you for the offer, but we shouldn't leave the bus unattended. I'll call and make arrangements for my kids, and we can sleep in the bus tonight."

Clearing her throat, Sister Prisha wasn't keen on the idea, but it wasn't her choice to make. "I'll go back and unlock the church, so you can use the facilities."

"Thank you, Sister Prisha. I think Courtney's right. We shouldn't leave the bus unattended." He didn't know if the hospital had procedures for situations like this, but he thought it was the right call. They had plenty of snacks to nibble on, and the backup battery power supply was fully charged. "I'll notify the hospital and keep them informed."

He mulled over the circumstance; most women would have been angered to find themselves stuck out in the middle of nowhere. Courtney was joking and laughing with the nuns as they walked toward the church to unlock the door. Never in his wildest dreams did he think he would find a woman like Courtney Clark both captivating and charming. With his thoughts still on Courtney, Blake walked to the bus to retrieve his cell phone to call the hospital.

***

They'd sat across from each other in the cockpit of the bus and talked into the wee hours of the morning. Not just chit-chat but deep meaningful conversation divulging their innermost thoughts —even revelations they'd never spoke, until now.

Courtney shared bits and pieces of her domestic abuse story and how her husband's death was still fresh after nearly two years. "There are days it feels like yesterday," she almost whispered. "When I hear of another opioid addiction death, classified as an accidental overdose, I weep. Josh's death came in his car, slumped over in the front seat. It was twenty-four hours before a Walmart employee noticed an unresponsive individual in the parking lot and called 911."

While Blake sat silently listening to Courtney, he recalled his conversation with his mother when he had whined about his first day on the job and being frustrated with the nursing assistant, and his mother emphasized, "*You just met this co-worker and you have no idea of this woman's personal circumstance. You never know what goes on behind closed doors.*" He was ashamed of his petulant behavior. He'd never imagined the courageous woman who sat across from him had endured such heartache.

"It wasn't accidental," she declared. "It was murder—fentanyl murdered the father of my children. There was no investigation into his death. The cartel and their dealers got to move on to their next client—the next victim."

With a sigh, she went silent. She realized that was the first time she'd expressed her deepest thoughts about the circumstance of Josh's death. She felt lighter. A secret burden had been lifted from her heavy heart. She felt she was in a safe place. She hoped she was right. She even thought she might even feel safe in Blake's arms.

Blake knew grieving over a lost marriage was devasting in itself, but then, in a short amount of time, enduring the death of your children's father in such devastating circumstances would be overwhelming for anyone to cope with, and Blake wondered how she could put one foot in front of the other.

"I'm so sorry for what you've endured."

It was only seven words, but Courtney appreciated the sincere brevity. *He really cares*, Courtney thought. She turned and their eyes met. She gave a soft smile. Her hopes rose.

As they sat in the dark, they didn't need to talk.

In the last few days of warm, autumn weather, the rhythm of high-pitched chirping crickets echoed in the night, until a gentle rainfall muffled their chirps.

"I just love the sound of rain," Courtney spoke softly. "It's so calming and soothing. It's a healing source for me." She closed her eyes to focus on the whispering sound. "My brain stops racing, my heartbeat slows, and I feel a sense of joy and peace." She paused searching for the best expression. "It's the little things in life that make me feel connected to God. It's like, my soul rests, listening to the voice of raindrops."

"I like that," Blake mused and smiled a little.

He repeated in his mind, *Listening to the voice of raindrops.*

"Good night," he said.

With eyes still closed, she bid him, "Sweet dreams." She drifted into sleep.

Blake could hear the pounding of his heart. He mused, *every time I hear the sound of rain, I'll think of Courtney.*

Courtney nodded off, but Blake couldn't sleep. Glancing over, he saw the moon's light fall softly, illuminating her face. It was angelic, and she looked beautiful. She'd used her coat as a blanket and pulled it up around her shoulders as she settled in the passenger's seat. He'd underestimated this strong woman. He wanted to reach over and stroke her hair, but he vanished the thought.

The first few days working together were bumpy, he'd admit he was mainly to blame. The inconvenient break down of the bus ended up being the invaluable circumstance that would mend their rift, and he'd realized he'd learned truths about Courtney—truths he'd never expected.

There was more to the happy-go-lucky, sugary sweet woman she'd portrayed to their patients. She'd experienced such a disappointing, troubled past. Now, as a single mom, she was rebuilding a happy life for herself and her children.

He sat for a while, looking at the night sky through the windshield. *Courageous*, he thought. When dreams shattered into nightmares, Courtney had the tenacious strength to protect her children. She'd begged God for help, and the Lord provided. On a wing and a prayer, she stepped out of a violent situation into the unknown and began her road to restoration. Wishing and praying for future happiness for her children. Earlier in the day, it baffled him when Courtney saw the nuns and said, 'God showed up.' But now, he understood—*God showed up in a mighty way.*

On her road to restoration, Blake knew that Courtney needed to feel safe, to build trust, and give herself permission and the freedom to move forward in life—to live again. He nodded off into a restless sleep, aspiring to be the man she could trust. The man who could renew her hope in love.

Blake woke in a cheerful mood, right up until he realized they were still out in the middle of nowhere and stuck in the mud.

Chapter Ten

Courtney concluded that the last few weeks had been the most challenging and the most rewarding, thus far, in her nursing assistant job. She was in seventh heaven to have four days off from work for the Thanksgiving holiday. She was exhausted, but she loved her work. To her, it wasn't so much a job; it was a calling.

She originally considered a nursing career because she liked caring for people—sometimes to a fault. She loved supporting her granny in the fears and confusion of dementia, volunteering at a pregnancy care center and helping a frightened single girl with an unplanned pregnancy, and staying awake twenty-four hours with a sick child. These experiences led to her first step in becoming a nursing assistant. She'd been a problem solver for as long as she could remember. When needed, she was always there. She'd sit quietly, listening, all the while finding a solution. It was just her nature.

She liked the additional responsibilities in her new role as a patients' advocate. In the beginning, her new title, Community Health Navigator, intimidated her but engaging with patients and facilitating additional needs, such as arranging transportation access for follow-up appointments, referrals for specialized services, and other individualized social needs, keep her connected to the patients throughout their care.

She knew what it was like to hurt, to be in physical and emotional pain, to live in fear. She also knew what it was like to accept kindness, compassion, and care from strangers. She wanted to be more like the Good Samaritan, the man from the Bible story, who went out of his way to help a wounded and bleeding stranger left on the side of the road to die. Offering a smile and a helping hand, she felt she was making a difference in the lives of others.

She sat in a rocking chair on the front porch, wrapped in a quilt, rocking and sipping her coffee, enjoying her quiet meditation before her children woke. It was Thanksgiving morning, and she was overwhelmed with God's blessings. She could never repay her father for his kindness in providing them with a home. Everything changed when they reconnected and when forgiveness broke the power of blame and cleansed her soul. In the last two years, she felt a freedom she'd never experienced. She felt reborn. Freedom from the anger and bitterness of her past. Freedom to live, to love, to be forgiven.

She never imagined the somewhat grouchy, good-looking man the dog lassoed on Halloween night would've become a romantic interest. It wasn't clear to her, just yet, whether Blake was a trick-or-treat. Either way, she enjoyed being his co-worker. And if she were being honest with herself, she wasn't sure if she was ready for a new love to be part of her story.

"Mom, what's for breakfast?" Chance peeked out the door, alerting Courtney to her mom duties.

"I'll be right in." She took one more gulp and headed indoors to flip some pancakes.

After breakfast, she had baking to do. She'd volunteered for dessert for the pitch-in Thanksgiving meal at Spring Valley Inn. After the Thanksgiving rehearsal dinner, two years prior for Shauna and Gabe's wedding, the feast became a family and friends' tradition. Chef Jean offered a classic Thanksgiving meal at noon for the guests and reserved the dining room for private dining in the evening.

Originally, Chef Jean insisted she prepare the meal, but eventually she gave in to the pitch-in idea with guests bringing their favorite holiday dish. It turned out to be a smorgasbord representing New England and Southern dishes. The traditional roast turkey, cranberry sauce, and pumpkin pie were staples of the meal. Chef Jean, raised in Boston, always had an oceanic twist to her dishes. You could count on her to serve clam chowder, oyster stuffing, and a seafood dip appetizer. This year, Ada planned to celebrate her Affrilachian roots by serving a gumbo of okra, corn, and tomatoes, and for an appetizer, Ada chose chitterlings, fried pork intestines doused in hot sauce. Courtney didn't know if she could handle the chitterlings, but she was glad Ada wasn't bringing one of her famous desserts since Courtney signed up for baking a Kentucky Jam Cake. There would be corn pudding, green bean casserole, mashed potatoes, gravy, candied yams, yeast rolls, and buttered biscuits. She gained five pounds just thinking about the menu.

With the breakfast plates in the dishwasher and the kids visiting Papaw Rich and Nana Alana, Courtney went from cupboard to cupboard pulling out the ingredients for her baking project.

She thumbed through her the recipe box and found the index card written in her grandmother's hand. Her eyes stung and her heart ached, but a smile spread across her face remembering Granny Runyon's kitchen, filled with spicy aromas of baking nutmeg mingled with cinnamon. Courtney could visualize her granny fluttering around the kitchen, busy as a bee, filled with excitement and anticipation because the holidays meant a house full of friends and family.

Growing up, Courtney didn't see her maternal, Runyon grandparents on a regular basis. Those visits were usually reserved for holidays. When Courtney's mom, Rachael, was a junior in high school, they'd decided to relocate from Bristol, Tennessee to Pikeville, Kentucky to be close to their extended family. Courtney's mom wanted to spend her senior year in Bristol, so she stayed behind and lived with friends.

When Courtney left home at eighteen, her Aunt Jessie invited Courtney to live with her family in Pikeville, where Courtney eventually met and married Joshua Clark. While living in Pikeville, she reconnected with Granny and Papaw Runyon.

They lived in a house tucked back in a holler. Courtney cherished time spent with them on their hilly homestead while they lived a simple life in retirement. Granny Runyon was a crazy chicken lady who spent most of her time talking to the chickens and tending to her grandchildren; she quilted until arthritis put an end to her craft. Papaw Runyon gave all of his attention to his huge garden he'd planted on the side of a hill; abundant rows filled with sweet corn, cucumbers, squash, white-half runner beans, and his prize-winning heirloom tomatoes were just a few of the vegetable he grew. Summers were spent with Granny Runyon bent over a hot stove, canning vegetables that would feed them through the long winter months. It was hard work, but Courtney contributed their longevity to their active lifestyle and dedication to hard work. They passed away before Courtney's children were born, and she wished they'd met their great-grandchildren.

She loved all of her grandparents and felt a pang of guilt, standing in her Granny Ramsey's kitchen. When Courtney walked away from her father, she'd also walked away from her paternal grandparents, sacrificing the loving relationship she had with them as a child. Growing up, she only visited with them a few times a year, but she loved them, and they loved her. She regretted severing that relationship. Eighteen-year-old children don't think about such things as consequences—until they grow up and have children of their own. She hoped they knew she loved them.

Courtney prided herself in keeping a clean house—that is, unless she was baking. She mirrored her Granny Runyon when it came to baking Kentucky Jam Cake and the mess left behind. Courtney left flour all over the countertops, utensils everywhere, and a sink full of mixing bowls. Granny's kitchen always looked as though the Pillsbury Doughboy exploded. She giggled when she remembered her papaw entering the kitchen and singing *When the Roll is Called Up Yonder* for the doughboy's funeral. He ended up with a dish towel in his face, but Courtney knew her granny loved his teasing nature.

She hoped she mirrored her granny in other ways. No matter who gathered around her Thanksgiving table, she greeted them with love and hospitality. Her generosity and kindness went beyond an Appalachian tradition; it was a love she mirrored from her Creator. Acceptance. Tolerance. A radiant love that gave her guests a sense of warmth and security.

It was no surprise, she thought, that during the holidays, the house became crowded with family who cherished Granny Runyon. Courtney would always lay the welcome mat out for her children and their future families. She wondered who would be gathered around her table when she held the title of grandmother.

***

The Spring Valley Inn was built in the late 1700's. Over the centuries, dignitaries and common folk had dined at the inn. Since the first meal was served, those walls echoed with the conversations and laughter of guests down through the ages. Today, friends and family would gather in the welcoming warmth of the dining room, adding dialogue to the echoes.

Chance opened the door to the kitchen; his mother and Gracie followed him inside. As expected, Chef Jean scurried around the room, barking orders to Craig, her sous chef, as they finished preparation for Thanksgiving dinner.

"Come in, come in," called Chef Jean. Always the consummate professional, she dressed in her chef's uniform of hat, white double-breasted jacket, black and white houndstooth pattern pants, and classic black clogs as she greeted her guests. "Happy Thanksgiving!" One by one she hugged the trio.

"Happy Thanksgiving!" Chance and Gracie responded in unison.

Courtney extended an air kiss to Chef Jean's cheek then placed her Jam Cake platter on the counter and scooted the kids into the dining room where Abby, Tyler, and the twins awaited.

Courtney, Gracie, Paige, and Bryce headed to the sitting room, adjacent to the dining room, where Nana Alana had a table arranged with fun activities for the children.

At Spring Valley Inn, Courtney always felt as if she were dining in a 5-Star resort. With Chef Jean's career as a culinary instructor and award-winning chef, combined with Alana's career in hotel management and experience from years working at luxury hotels, the inn brought a sophisticated charm to the community. A white linen tablecloth, fine china, and crystal dressed the classic Victorian mahogany dining table with spiral legs. Twelve matching balloon-back, linen-upholstered, cushion chairs awaited guests. From the dramatic, large-blooming magnolia flowers on a black background wallpaper to the classic vintage crystal candle chandelier, the decor spoke luxurious elegance. An autumn floral and gourd grapevine swag adorned the fireplace mantle. A watercolor rendering of the downtown buildings of Spring Valley hung over the mantle. The artist's depiction captured the charm of the little town. Federal, Greek Revival, and Victorian style homes lined the streets that led to the historic downtown district. A scattering of light reflecting from the chandelier gave the painting a luminous effect— as if the sidewalk glowed. Shoppers walked on the historic brick sidewalks. The uneven appearance, cracks, and gaps were so beautiful. Soft music played in the background. The aroma of fall wafted from the pumpkin spice scented candles on the mantle.

The vintage doorbell, a whimsical, brass, decorative owl perched on a branch that held the little bell, rang announcing the arrival of Ada and J.R. Ada couldn't help herself, she had to say it, "Every time a bell rings, an angel gets its wings." The rest of the dinner guests, except one, followed them inside to the dining room. Servers bustled around with hot food and drinks as everyone talked and laughed and caught up with old friends and family.

Courtney had felt anxious all morning. It was silly, she thought, but she was nervous. She kept reminding herself she wasn't seeking romance, and Blake would be moving on to his next assignment in a few weeks, probably never to be seen again. But she couldn't shake it off.

Nervy, Courtney glanced toward the stairwell as Blake came down the stairs two at a time. Even in his scrubs, she'd always considered him attractive, but today, he made her heart skitter. He still held that coastal town, carefree, and adventurous vibe but sharpened his look with a lightweight, athletic fit, navy jacket with high collar, patch pockets, and button closures worn over a long sleeve, light blue crewneck shirt and jeans. She'd describe it as modern Southern preppiness. As usual, he habitually ran his fingers through his mussed-up, sun-streaked hair, which drove her crazy. When their eyes met, he smiled.

She melted.

Chapter Eleven

B lake thought of Courtney as he dressed for the evening. He found it perplexing— they were getting along so well. The mutual attraction wasn't his imagination. Even though they had met only a short time ago, he felt as if he'd known her for a lifetime. He'd never felt a closer bond to any woman he'd ever met. Ordinarily, the next step should come easy. Why did it seem so difficult?

Maybe he was overthinking the situation, he considered. Maybe he needed to back off a little. He'd take one day at a time and see how things progressed, he resolved.

He caught Courtney's glance, smiled, and gave her a long, considering look as he descended the staircase. Courtney seemed delighted to see him and made Blake forget his perplexing relationship quandary.

While Courtney dealt with situating the children at the kids' table and helping arrange dishes on the crowded dining table, Blake chatted with Gabe and Tyler. Ada sought Blake out and introduced him to J.R., her husband. Ada's lighthearted chatter made Blake comfortable with a room full of new acquaintances. Following brief re-introductions, Chef Jean announced dinner was served and requested guests find their place card, assigned seating.

Courtney took Blake's arm and whispered in his ear, "You're with me."

He liked the sound of those words from her; *you're with me*.

"Thank the good Lord," he murmured. He enjoyed chatting with Ada, but he had visions of their last conversation in the coffee shop where he couldn't get a word in edge wise. But even if he had been seated by Ada, he wouldn't complain. Holidays summoned homesickness. Blake had thought about driving home to spend Thanksgiving with his family, but he would have spent more time driving than visiting. He'd discussed it with his parents, and they agreed. He'd planned on dining at the inn alone, but when Chef Jean extended the invitation to join family and friends, he willingly accepted. The invite scattered the homesick feeling.

As everyone gathered around the table, Blake thought it felt a lot like home. There was a genuine love and acceptance for one another, memories were being made, the bond of new and old friendship united as one, and laughter was endless. Today, he was grateful for the blessings of new friendships and especially grateful for the woman who sat next to him. The unexpected blessing God had provided.

His grateful mood continued throughout

the evening as he dined with Courtney by his side. It wasn't just food. The amazing meal was an assortment of cuisine connecting people of different backgrounds and regions of the country. With Ada's relentless coaxing, Blake even took a bite of her chitterlings. Strange, funky, and with a buttery texture, he compared them to octopus and complimented Ada on her dish. Courtney's Kentucky Jam Cake was Blake's favorite on the dessert table. Courtney watched as he took his first bite. From the sparkle in her eye, Blake was confident his reaction pleased her.

The spice cake with a touch of tartness from blackberries and the sweet, lightly salty caramel frosting spread on top was pure heaven. It reminded him of his grandmother's spice cake. "It tastes like home," he murmured with his mouth full.

After dessert, Gabe stood to make an announcement.

"First, I want to officially welcome our two new guests this year, Blake and Arrow. We're glad you could join this rowdy clan." Everyone broke out in applause. Romance had finally knocked on Jean's door—his name was Arrow. Chef Jean beamed as she cuddled up next to Arrow, whom she preferred to call her *mon amour*. My love. Jean, and everyone else, secretly hoped a Christmas proposal was in the making.

"Secondly, Ada has a request. Before she takes the floor, I want to remind you that the

Giving Tree project brought us all together, and I have a sneaky suspicion she has a special request up her sleeve."

Ada scooted her seat back and stood. "The last two years, I've called on you to fulfill big requests from the Giving Tree project, and you've always gone above and beyond. But, I have to warn you, I've got a doozy of a request that's going to take an army of volunteers." She took a sip of her water and dabbed her sweaty brow with her napkin. "A lady stopped by the coffee house telling me about their church trying to help out four families who were flood victims at the beginning of this past year. They were denied FEMA trailers for temporary housing, so their small congregation was able to pull together their resources and provide travel trailers and parked them in the church parking lot. The church folk are tapped out financially and wondered if we could provide Christmas gifts for the four families."

Blake turned to look at Courtney. "This sounds familiar, doesn't it?" She nodded her head.

"Ada, excuse me," Courtney spoke, "but we think we know who you're talking about. One of the locations for the Health Bus is that church parking lot. We saw the travel trailers and chatted with a volunteer from the church who filled us in on the situation."

"Oh, thank goodness. I'm so glad to hear you say that. I'm a trusting soul, but it was such a big request. I was going to ask if someone would investigate and confirm the state of affairs."

"There's definitely a real need. The stories we heard were devastating," Blake concurred. "I would be more than willing to help out any way I can."

"Bless your heart, and thank you so much! And remember, the launch for the Giving Tree project is this Sunday evening at the coffee house, and I would love to have everyone in attendance for the official assignment of projects." Before she took a seat, Ada continued, "Shauna, will you take on organizing the task at hand? I'll provide you with all the information so you can assign jobs."

"Absolutely! I think I have everyone's cell numbers and email addresses except Blake and Arrow." She looked over their way. "Don't forget to give me your info before you leave tonight."

Colleen, Shauna's mother, and owner of the Old Towne Christmas Shop, volunteered to provide Christmas decorations. "Since I'm sure space is limited in the travel trailers, I have tabletop Christmas trees with LED lights, pinecones, balls, and red berries hanging ornaments I will donate."

One by one, every person around the table volunteered for the Giving Tree project.

Gabe clinked his glass to gather everyone's attention. He nodded for Shauna to join him at the head of the table. "We also have an announcement to make." He grinned from ear to ear. In unison they excitedly announced, "We're having a baby!"

Shauna caressed her belly.

Cheerfully, everyone clapped, including Blake. He'd admit he was a softy when it came to babies. He was caught, more than once, wiping away tears when he was involved in a delivery. He found babies were so huggable and absolutely adorable—a wonderful gift from God.

A pure river of joy flowed from the expectant parents' hearts. He watched as tears that swam in their eyes freely spilled over. In loving embrace, the sisters jumped in excitement, and grown men hugged unabashedly. He'd never seen a happier group of people. He was honored to be celebrating this special moment with his new friends on this blessed Thanksgiving Day.

***

The sound of laughter drifted away as dinner guests packed up their empty dishes and called it a night. As earlier arranged, Papaw Rich took Chance and Gracie home, while Alana and Courtney volunteered to be part of the clean-up crew. Blake pitched in until Alana insisted that he and Courtney retreat to the lobby for after-dinner coffee.

Behind the half-circle, rich mahogany executive desk was one, of many, ornate fireplaces in the inn. The dramatic watercolor painting above the mantle demanded Blake's attention. The stunning piece captured wild rhododendrons that decorated the landscape in Appalachian highlands. The deep green leaves with beautiful, large, trumpet-shaped, and frilly white blossoms were striking. He could almost feel the ray of sunlight reflecting off the foliage.

"Isn't it beautiful?" Courtney's voice was soft and genuine. "It's so realistic, sometimes, I swear I can smell it's sweet fragrance."

"It's brilliant. Who's the incredible artist?"

"Jeff Chapman-Crane. He's a renowned Appalachian artist. He focuses his art on the culture of Appalachia. He's a master at depicting the life and the land in the mountains. His portrait work is just as marvelous as his landscapes. I think he captures the soul of man and nature on canvas."

"I'll Google him to see more of his work. He is a skillful craftsman."

"Better yet, he and his wife have a gallery in Eolia, Kentucky. If you ever want to take a road trip, it's only about a two-hour drive from here," Courtney suggested. "The Gallery hours are by appointment only, so we'd have to schedule in advance."

"Sounds like you've visited the gallery."

"I have. Alana wanted to feature more Appalachian artists at the inn. I went with Dad and Alana when they purchased this piece."

Courtney helped herself to a cup of coffee from the hospitality table. "Can I interest you in a cup?"

"No, I'm good, but thank-you."

They were alone. Dinner guests had said their good-byes, and the hotel guests had retired to their rooms. The original parlor that now served as a check-in lobby was dimly lit with two lamps casting a soft glow. It was quiet, except for the occasional sound of clanking dishes resonating from the kitchen and a car passing by outside on Main Street. Blake felt it was a pleasant, warm, and cozy atmosphere. He'd enjoyed the evening with new friends around the dinner table, but all night he'd longed to spend a few minutes alone with Courtney. It had been so long since he'd felt this way. He wondered, could she be the one who would fill the loneliness and heal his wounded heart? And would he be the man she needed, the man she could trust with herself and her children? He questioned himself, his heart, and his motives. Would he be strong enough for a complicated relationship? Was he foolish to think he could be hers?

Courtney took a seat on the elegant, pale blue, velvet, Victorian loveseat and comfortably tucked one leg under the other as she watched Blake still admiring the painting.

Blake turned his attention toward Courtney. The delight in her eyes would have had any man take a seat beside her. The couch could easily be shared, but very intimate seating. After all, the loveseat was originally designed for courting couples. *Were they courting?* he pondered. Remembering his decision to slow things down, Blake chose the leather wingback chair and sat across from her as she settled back and sipped her coffee. With the backdrop of the Victorian English Regency furniture, she held an air of elegance and romance, he thought. Blake sometimes wondered if she was aware of her natural, effortless beauty that he'd been admiring all evening.

"Did I ever tell you I dabble in watercolor?"

"No, you haven't mentioned that you're an artist. You're a man of many mysteries." Courtney drew her cup to her lips and sipped wondering what other secret talents this man held.

"My grandmother is a watercolor artist and quite well known in the Outer Banks for her beach landscapes. I was around eight years old when she introduced me to her craft. She was sneaky. She started by having me help her drag her portable painting easel over sand dunes one summer and then set up my own easel. She eventually got me hooked on art."

"Someday, you'll have to show me your work. I would love to see it."

"I'm working on a project in my room. When it's time to unveil, I'll have a personal showing. I expect it to be unveiled by Christmas."

"You've piqued my curiosity. Is it a landscape or portrait?"

"I'll keep that my little secret. You'll have to wait for the unveiling," he teased. He actually had two ongoing projects, and one painting was for Courtney.

For a long time, they conversed in casual conversation, tossing around ideas for the Giving

Tree project, unique Christmas gifts to send his family, his watercolor hobby, and upcoming holiday events in Spring Valley.

"The annual Christmas parade is tomorrow night. The best seats in town are on the inn's upstairs balcony. You want us to save you a seat?" she asked, anticipating a favorable response. Her eyes still held delight and warmth. "That is, if you don't already have plans." She smiled, giving him a way out if he so chose.

He grinned. "Absolutely! I love a good parade." *Maybe they were in the early stages of courting after all,* he thought. He was going to ask her on a date soon, so he'd consider this their first social engagement. "It's a date!" he stated unwaveringly.

"Perfect!" Courtney replied, nervously tucking her hair behind her ear. His response was as she had hoped. But qualifying saving a seat for the parade as a date was a little unsettling. She couldn't remember ever asking a guy out on a date before. She'd held a little shield against romance, but maybe it was time to abandon her defense. Day by day her attraction for him grew. She'd hoped it was only a matter of time before he would ask her out on a date, but this would suffice. She surmised, since she'd made the first move, she was now a modern woman. She sheepishly grinned at the thought.

Alana peeked around the kitchen door and almost whispered, "Hate to interrupt, but are you ready to drive home?"

"Oh, my goodness!" Courtney looked at the time. "I didn't realize it was so late." She jumped up and reached for her jacket that hung on the coat tree.

A true Southern gentleman, Blake rose and helped Courtney with her jacket. He stood close behind her and held the coat open as she reached her arms back and found the armholes.

Courtney was capable of putting on her own jacket, but it was impossible not to enjoy the unavoidable romantic undertones as the fabric slowly brushed over her skin, and Blake gently lifted her hair from under the collar. She turned to face him. They stood for a moment, eyes locked on each other. Courtney tilted her head. Her voice became ever so slightly softer. "Thank you. I guess I'll see you tomorrow at the parade."

"You can count on it." In that moment, he imagined running his hand over her cheek and their lips meeting. His imagination remained in his head, but he sensed she knew his thoughts. He took a deep breath and backed away.

As she walked toward the door, she turned, smiled, and waved goodbye to him. Courtney disappeared behind the door, and Blake immediately felt an overwhelming sense of emptiness. He realized that without her, life would be empty—there would always be loneliness. He didn't want to think about it. For a moment, he stood staring at the door, entangled in a barrage of emotions. He didn't want to be without her, Blake sighed. He asked himself, *what are you going to do about it?* Lost in thought, his halting steps led him up the stairs to his room. He didn't have the answer, but he would work on it like his life—like his happiness—depended upon it.

Chapter Twelve

Courtney thought there was nothing like Christmas in Spring Valley, except for the 4th of July weekend or Halloween or Easter. The townsfolk definitely knew how to celebrate holidays.

Christmas in Spring Valley wasn't designated to just one weekend; instead, it was a month-long celebration with the Appalachian Heritage Christmas Festival, escorted in by the annual Christmas parade on Friday night and the tree lighting on Saturday. The town came alive with the parade festivities. Tourists literally were bused in, due to limited downtown parking.

The historic town drew thousands of visitors during the holidays. Local artisans capitalized on the welcomed bombardment, offering their finest handcrafted Appalachian folk art celebrating their heritage. The calendar was filled with family activities like the parade, the Dog Gone Days pet costume competition, various tree lightings, a church stroll, and the fan-favorite Santa Train Depot.

Courtney watched Alana ready the inn's lobby where the naked balsam fir tree stood, awaiting to be adorned with hand-carved, whimsical, wooden ornaments. It was a tradition at the inn for guests to gather after the parade and trim the tree. Alana wanted to make guests feel at home and get everyone in the holiday spirit. Courtney was surprised that the spicy scent of a recently harvested tree filled the air.

"Is it my imagination, or does that artificial tree smell like a live tree?"

"Your mind isn't playing tricks on you." Alana peeked around a dark green branch. "I'm a little afraid to use a live tree, due to the fire hazard. The inn has survived three fires in its history, and I don't want to push my luck."

"What's your secret?" Courtney inhaled the rich, warm aroma.

"It's a fragrance oil I spritzed on the tree." She stood back a few feet to see if the tree was unswerving. "Doesn't it remind you of a weekend walk in the woods? I just love it!"

"It smells like Christmas!"

"Where are the grandkids?"

"They're with Abby and the twins at the Olde Towne Christmas shop making secret gifts."

"That sounds like fun. Are they going to be able to stay and help decorate the tree after the parade?"

"Absolutely, I would have a mutiny on my hands if we changed plans."

Courtney reminisced of how Alana had been instrumental in reuniting her with her father. Even though Alana and Rich were in the early stages of their romance, Alana welcomed Courtney and her children into her life with open arms. It would have been natural, Courtney thought, for Alana to want Rich all to herself, definitely less complicated for the new couple, but Alana unselfishly put Rich's needs before her own. Courtney remembered Alana saying, *isn't that what love is all about*?

"I heard you may have a free night tonight?" Alana quizzed her daughter-in-heart.

"I do. After the tree decorating, Gabe and Shauna are having a big sleepover at the cabin with Chance, Gracie, Paige, and Bryce. Tomorrow morning, they have a hike planned, and then they'll be back here for pics with Santa." Courtney snickered, "I hope they know what they've gotten themselves into."

"They'll be fine. Gabe's been hosting summer camps with a lot more kids than four to deal with. Maybe this will give you and Blake some alone time." Alana gave her a sly grin and raised her eyebrows.

"Seems like everyone is ganging up on me in this matchmaking game y'all have goin' on." Courtney didn't want to jump into this conversation and started toward the door. "It's about time to pick up the kids and grab a bite to eat before the parade."

Before she could escape, Alana walked over and gave Courtney a big hug. "There's just something magical about Christmas. Love is in the air. I just don't want you to miss out on a special opportunity. No pressure, just have an open heart."

That was exactly what Courtney was afraid of—to open her heart.

***

The excitement in the air was electrifying as onlookers lined Main Street and carols rang out from a church steeple's loudspeaker. They had the bird's-eye view from the balcony of the inn for this family affair. It was all Courtney could do to keep Gracie, Chance, and the twins from jumping off the balcony. They saved a rocking chair for Blake where he'd made himself comfortable.

Courtney leaned over and whispered in Blake's ear, "Remember, Gracie and Chance don't know that their grandfather is also Father Christmas, and that's the way we want to keep it."

"Your secret is safe with me."

Snow flurries started flying, but it didn't bother the crowd. The swirling flakes made for a perfect snow globe experience. The children held their heads back with mouths open wide to catch the falling crystals.

"Snowflakes are kisses from heaven," Gracie giggled.

The fleeting flurries disappeared almost as quickly as they came, but the activity kept the kids busy until the sounds of the marching band echoed down Main Street.

The parade was a historical timeline. The entries included a blend of old-fashioned exhibits for the nostalgia folk and a glittering holiday experience with twinkling lights and glitz for the younger generation. As tradition, and a central part of the community, the high school marching band and the flag corps twirling their flags led the parade with beloved, lively holiday tunes. The talented students were followed by decorated floats, all vying to take home the coveted award of Best in Parade in the annual competition.

"Look, Mom, it's Daniel Boone!" Chance admired the adventures of the early frontiersman almost as much as pirates.

The float depicted Boone and early settlers who'd adventured across the Appalachian Mountains to hunt and explore. Dressed in buckskin leggings, moccasin boots, fringed shirt, a wide-brimmed-beaver-felt hat, and carrying a long rifle, Daniel Boone waved at the crowd. The woman depicting Rebecca Boone was dressed in a simple Quaker-style long brown dress, and an apron tied around her waist met the hem of her garment. She covered her hair with a bonnet tied under her chin. She swaddled an infant in her arms. Courtney couldn't imagine the trials that Rebecca Boone endured in those frontier days.

"I need to get a selfie with Daniel since I'm a descendant," Blake enlightened the group.

"I wondered, when you first introduced yourself as Blake Boone, if you had any connection, but I didn't think it polite to ask," Courtney responded.

"Why not?"

"If you weren't, I'm sure you'd be tired of people asking, so I didn't," Courtney explained. "You said you could trace your ancestry back to the shipwrecked English, Scottish-Irish immigrants in the early colonies. I don't remember Daniel Boone roaming the Outer Banks."

"My paternal ancestry traces back to Squire Boone in North Carolina. Mom and Dad met in college and ended up back in Nags Head. Mom always said I get my wanderlust from my dad's side of the family."

Courtney's thinking became encircled in his words as his comment twinged her heart. She only hoped his lust for wandering would wane.

"I'm like Chance. When I was a little boy, I thought it was cool, but I never got caught up in my ancestry. Now, my sisters love that stuff. They've even been to the annual Daniel Boone Festival in Mocksville, North Carolina."

"I've found in my own life that when I explored my family history, learning their stories gave me a better understanding of myself. Afterall, every step they took led to me. Because of my search, I know what I am now. I'm a mountain woman," Courtney shared with pride. "Well, you're in Boone country, so you'll have to visit one of the 'Boone Bear Trees' where Daniel Boone killed a bear and carved the date and his name in the bark. The tree is gone, but there's a historical marker, and I think just knowing that multiple generations back, your famous ancestor stood on the same ground is incredible."

Blake felt a tinge of guilt. Daniel Boone was one of the first and most famous folk heroes in America. The topic made for easy conversations and gave him a quip for not settling down—it was the DNA wanderer that flowed through his blood. But it also provided hours of endless teasing growing up. If he had a dollar for every time some kid asked if he wore a coonskin cap, he'd be a wealthy man. He considered that maybe he'd shied away from delving into his ancestry for fear of not being able to live up to the legend. Maybe it was time for him to really start exploring his family tree and discover how the past shaped his journey.

"Let's schedule an afternoon where we can take the kids and get a selfie beside the monument."

"It's a date," Courtney smiled. Joy bubbled up in her, but she said nothing out loud. She liked that he suggested including her children in an outing.

Sitting side by side and sharing a blanket, Blake reached over to link hands with Courtney. She turned to face him. A smile bloomed. She squeezed his hand in approval and cuddled closer. Blake felt his heart healing. He hadn't celebrated Christmas like this in years. After his break-up, he'd always been away, working with strangers, and missed out on holiday festivities with family.

He wasn't home, but Blake thought it sure felt like family.

Chapter Thirteen

S hortly before ten, Blake stepped outside into the nippy air. Friday night while the town slept, Jack Frost had paid a visit. Ice crystals still glistened on shadowed portions of the sidewalk—the first manifestation of winter. Overnight, it seemed as though the town woke with Christmas fever.

His destination was on the opposite end of town. Churches bookended Main Street. He grinned and thought of the scripture, *the Lord's blessing you on your comings and goings.* He passed dozens of shoppers getting a jump on the Christmas rush. Couples strolled hand-in-hand "window-shopping," oohing and aahing at the holiday displays. He walked down the brick paved sidewalks that were lined by garland trimmed lampposts and adorned with gingham-ribbon-bowed wreaths that cradled red vintage oil lanterns in their center. In the courthouse yard towered a huge and lackluster Christmas tree, wrapped with colored lights that zigzagged up and down the tree, scattered red bows were tied to branches. It looked drab in the daylight, but the tree would come alive with sparkling, dancing lights later that evening at the Tree Lighting

Ceremony, illuminating the holiday festivities with all its magic and glory. He wondered if Spring Valley had ever been approached to be a filming location set for a cozy holiday romance movie.

For Blake, Christmastime had lost some of its childhood magic. Adulting required reality living. His chosen career path didn't prioritize holidays, so Christmas became just another workday. He missed the magic of the holidays.

As he approached the entrance of the Old Towne Christmas Shop, there stood a rustic, life-sized Santa Claus figure, twisted hickory walking stick in-hand. A heart-shaped face barn owl perched on his shoulder, evoking an Appalachian Trail Father Christmas aura.

The jolly old elf was dressed in a vintage-burnished burgundy, ankle-length robe. A folk-art masterpiece. The eye-catching Santa captured Blake's attention, and he stopped for moment to admire the skill of the artist. The piece was charmingly recreated from the top of its brown, fur-trimmed and hooded robe to its leather-strapped, black-buckled boots.

The hand sculpted, expressive face was so lifelike, Blake would've sworn its lips moved, and its piercing, blue eyes twinkled.

This Christmas, Blake thought, maybe Santa would gift him a little magic. After all, wasn't it, *the most wonderful time of the year*?

He wished he still believed in Santa.

It shouldn't be much further, Blake

estimated, to his final destination. He continued on.

***

The spinning red, white, and blue striped barber pole signified he'd found the right place. Bluegrass Barbershop sat on Main Street cozy between a candy store and a cigar shop. You could get a trim, chocolate, and a stogie, all in one trip. The building looked no bigger than a spacious walk-in closet.

From the moment he stepped in the door and whiffed the distinct citrus and musky aroma, Blake knew this would be no ordinary visit to the barber. He could barely squeeze in the room because a group of musicians with banjo, guitar, and mandolin plucked away on bluegrass tunes. Blake wasn't sure which person was the barber until the guitar player made eye contact and spoke over the music.

"Come on in. You can have a seat in the barber chair. We've got a few more bars in this tune, and I'll be right with you." The barber continued plucking the strings.

The classic barber chair looked as old as the historic building that housed the shop. Relieved, Blake found it reliable and comfortable as he sat back and enjoyed the bluegrass music. He even caught himself tapping his toe. When the barber finished the song, he draped a cape around Blake and listened to his new client's hairstyle request. All the while, the musicians turned the sound down a notch or two to accommodate conversation and continued to entertain the only customer. If Blake could afford to have any band give him a private concert, he wouldn't have chosen bluegrass, but he found himself enjoying the private show that would only cost him the price of a haircut.

"It's quite an interesting place you have here." New and used instruments lined the walls. "Do you play in a bluegrass band when you're not cutting hair?"

"No, I get all the playin' I need here in the shop." The barber began trimming Blake's hair with scissors. "Been here going on thirty years. In the down time, I'd just play a few tunes on different instruments." Snip, snip. More hair fell to the floor. "Originally, the name of the barbershop was, Boodle's Barbershop. That's my nickname, but when my music buddies started stoppin' in for a cut and afterwards grabbed my instruments to jam for a few minutes, it became a local tradition, and I changed the name to Bluegrass Barbershop."

Talking over the music, they chatted. The barber told him about his sidekicks, Neal, Bug, and Corbin and how they'd been entertaining customers for years. Boodle joked, "These guys are like brothers, except they don't fight or consider me their personal ATM."

Boodle must have assumed his client didn't know many bluegrass tunes and yelled over, "Fellas, play one that everybody knows."

He assumed correctly. Blake wasn't that

familiar with the music genre, but he recognized what the gentlemen began picking when they broke into the iconic song, "Foggy Mountain Breakdown." The last tune confirmed it; there's was no way a person would leave the shop without spirits being lifted.

Blake had to concentrate to not move around in the chair to the beat. He just wanted a trim and didn't want to chance losing a chunk of hair. There wasn't a lot of talking going on, but there was a whole lot of toes tapping.

When Gabe referred Blake to the barbershop, he grinned and warned Blake that he was in for a unique experience. Gabe undersold the experience. It was incredible. This local hangout was an Appalachia cultural encounter.

Some might find Spring Valley too quirky; others would find it charming. Blake found himself thinking that he could get used to this charming, quirky place.

***

Pleased with his haircut, he left the barbershop on a high note. The previous evening, Blake overheard that Courtney planned to take the kids to the Santa Train Depot for pictures. As it was only a few minutes' walk to the Train Depot, he decided he'd take his chances and see if they had arrived.

As he walked on, he spied the little family all bundled in coats, scarfs, and gloves. Courtney, Chance, Gracie, and the dog and cat, both on leashes, were leaving the Olde Town Christmas

Shop and heading toward the Train Depot. He sped up his pace and joined the little family. He lightly bumped Courtney's shoulder to let her know she had company. She almost dropped the venti coffee cup she was sipping. Annoyed, she jerked around to see who invaded her space.

Courtney was pleasantly surprised. "Fancy seeing you here."

Blake ran his fingers through his choppy hair. "I visited the barbershop and thought I'd roam around town to see what's happening." Blake motioned toward the pets, "What's on the agenda?"

"Pics with the pets at Santa's Train Depot. You're welcome to join us if you can handle long lines, crazy children, perky elves, and a whole lot of Ho, Ho, Ho's."

"I'm all in. Can't wait."

She whispered, "Just a reminder, the kids don't know Papaw Rich is Santa, so keep it under wraps."

"You swore me to secrecy last night. You don't have to keep reminding me. I promise, your secret is safe with me, even though, if my grandfather were Santa, that would be the coolest."

"You do realize he's just filling in for Father Christmas, don't you?"

"I know, but it would still be really cool."

"Not a word, promise?"

"Scout's honor." He lifted a hand in a Boy

Scout salute.

"I bet you weren't even in the Boy Scouts."

"Hey, I'm trustworthy, and…and, prepared. That's it." She was correct. He was pulling words from scenes from one of his favorite TV shows, *3rd Rock from the Sun*, in the episode where Harry attempted to follow the ways of the Boy Scouts. As a twelve-year-old, he thought the show was hilarious.

She didn't speak, but she thought, *Trust is complicated.* She didn't have the greatest track record in the trust department. For her, having trust was imperative in a relationship, and Blake seemed trustworthy, Courtney contemplated. She didn't know him well enough to make that determination. *But how do you really know? Am I willing to take the risks? Only time would tell.*

They walked close together side by side; he took her hand. Courtney lifted her eyes to his and just smiled at Blake. She felt something unexpected—happiness.

***

As forewarned, Christmas spirit was alive and well at the Santa Train Depot brimming with families dressed in ugly sweaters and holiday-themed pajamas, and pets in costumes all anxiously awaiting their turn to whisper their wishes in the ear of the jolly gift-giver. Welcoming all to the depot, an eye-catching magical holiday décor of lighted reindeer and a sleigh sat on the roof of the bright red, restored caboose, signaling that Santa awaited just inside the railroad car.

Teens dressed in red and green playful-elves costumes handed out number cards to reserve a spot with Santa. "Looks like we'll be here for a while," Courtney said as she showed Blake the number fourteen.

An elf directed them to the historic Railroad Depot-turned-Santa's Village set up for a while-you-wait family fun center including ornament decorating, face painting, storytelling, and a handy stocking stuffer gift shop to get a jump start on holiday shopping.

"Mom, I can't handle Nick on a leash and make ornaments at the same time. Would you hold him?" Chance held out the dog's leash to Courtney.

"I have a better idea, if you and Gracie promise to be good and stay inside until we come and get you for pictures, Blake and I will take Nick and Angel outside."

Just as they were ready to promise, Abby and the twins greeted them. Abby suggested, "I'll watch the kids. You two go on outside. If you hurry, there's an empty bench."

Gracie handed Blake the cat's leash. He leaned over and whispered to Courtney, "As soon as we get outside, we're switching. I can't be seen with a cat on a leash."

"Are you worried Gracie's fur baby won't cooperate, or are you too manly to be seen walking a cat?" Courtney teased.

"Actually, both."

"Then you'll really be embarrassed when we dress them in costumes." She reached in her backpack and pulled out a reindeer antlers headband and a pet bow tie collar for Nick and an adorable red Santa hat and collar with jingle bells for Angel.

Blake dropped his head in total bewilderment.

Courtney's eyes danced with laughter as she slid him a glance. "Just a reminder, a corgi is not considered one of the manliest dog breeds. So, either pet you choose, you may take a hit to your masculinity."

"Give me the dog leash." He grinned at Courtney, "It's the least damaging."

Courtney swapped leashes as she took the lead and walked outside to the bench. Blake followed with a rear view of the feisty, chubby corgi as Nick shimmied his fluffy behind. In the excitement the small pup barked to let everyone know what was going on. He also liked to be in charge and, even on a leash, attempted to herd the crowd. Blake determined that the corgi had a Napoleon complex. He thought to himself, *the things you do for love.*

***

As Courtney neared the bench, she suddenly realized it was the exact same bench she'd occupied two Christmases ago when her life was in turmoil and seemed hopeless. Desperate, afraid, despondent, and lonely, she didn't know then, but she knew now that it was a divine appointment to have her kids picture made with the Spring Valley Santa. Unbeknownst to her then, Santa was her estranged father. That day changed their lives forever. She wondered if meeting up with Blake today was also a divine appointment. She got a warm and fuzzy feeling, thinking that this might just turn out to be an absolutely perfect Christmas.

***

The kids finished decorating their ornaments in Santa's Village and joined Courtney and Blake outside at the bench just in time for when an elf called out their number. Gracie clapped in excitement, Nick barked, and Angel the cat, wearing her antler headband, took the opportunity to flop over and freeze. "Mom, she won't budge." Gracie whined as she pulled on the cat's leash.

"Honey, just pick her up and carry her. She'll be fine." Courtney encouraged her daughter as she scooted the motley crew up the steps of the red caboose toward Santa, who had the appearance of royalty while sitting on his custom-made chair. It looked like a tall, wooden, high-back throne, decorated with elves, toys, and a Santa engraving carved in the wood. The backrest and seat were covered with green velvet upholstery.

As she unbundled the kids' jackets to reveal their Christmas sweaters, Courtney convinced herself that there was no way her children would recognize their grandfather. The self-proclaimed over-fifty-and-fit club member had metamorphosed into the legendary Santa Claus, the portly, white-bearded man with spectacles. He was wearing a deep-red velvet jacket with faux-fur trim, white-fur-cuffed red trousers, a red hat with white fur, a black leather belt, and boots. An eye-catching, custom-made belt buckle, hand-painted in brilliant colors, depicted a nativity scene.

"I'm digging his belt buckle," Gabe was impressed.

"Dad had it special made as a little reminder that Christmas is all about God's gift of love."

"Need I remind you? That's not your dad, it's Santa." Blake leaned over close to assure her as if he knew her thoughts. "But from the looks of things, I think the corgi knows your secret." They watched as the pup jumped excitedly on Santa's lap anticipating that Papaw Rich would feed him a treat. "It's a good thing that dogs can't talk, otherwise the jig is up," Blake teased.

"Calm down, Nick." The holly jolly fellow petted the feisty corgi and dug a treat out of his giant pocket.

Bewildered, Chance looked at Santa. "How do you know his name?"

Tapping the side of his nose while looking Chance in the eyes, he whispered, "Santa knows all your names!" He let out a belly laugh followed by a hearty "Ho, ho, ho!"

Courtney thought that his robust laugh would charm anyone, even non-believers.

With only a few minutes allotted for the photo shoot, the playful elves took control and went into full work mode posing the children and the wiggly, energetic pets around Santa. In rapid fire, the photographer took multiple shots guaranteed to capture at least one perfect moment.

As Courtney and Blake took control of the pets and chose the best shot, Gracie and Chance had their private chat with the mythical wish-giver. Chance went first describing in detail his wish. When he finished, Gracie whispered something in Santa's ear. Courtney watched as Santa leaned in and chatted with Gracie, and then she shook her head in agreement like she understood him. She put her finger on her chin in deep thought and sat for a moment then whispered in his ear for the second time. He gave her the thumbs up, and she gave the jolly old elf a kiss on the cheek. They waved goodbye and joined Courtney and Blake.

After they exited the railroad car when Courtney helped Gracie with her jacket, she asked about the long discussion with Santa.

"Don't worry, Mom. I wasn't asking for a bunch of stuff. The first wish he said wasn't in his department and that he couldn't grant it. He said it was something he called a *blessing,* and I needed to pray about it." Gracie looked a little confused as she continued, "He said that Santa takes care of wishes like toys. So, I asked for a toy."

"Are you disappointed?"

"No, I'll just ask God for the blessing and see what happens."

"Just remember, not all prayers are answered the way we hope." Courtney didn't want to discourage her daughter, but she had no idea what was on Gracie's mind. Courtney had an intimate relationship with the Lord and experienced first-hand the joy, power, and miracles of prayer, but she also knew she didn't want her children to think that prayer was like rubbing a lamp for a genie to pop out and grant wishes.

The comment didn't dampen Gracie's hopeful spirit. She looked up at her mother with a big smile and said, "We'll see." As they left the train depot, Gracie cozied between Courtney and Blake. She took their hands and walked together toward the Spring Valley Inn for cookies and cocoa, and started praying for a blessing.

Chapter Fourteen

aylight had almost faded. Twilight rays of shadowing light kept the path from being completely dark. Ada felt it meditative—somewhere between heaven and earth. The sweet scent of a magnificent, flowering magnolia hung in the air. She stopped briefly at the incredible trunk, under the low, dense canopy, contemplating how she now stood in the exact same spot where hundreds of years ago, her people once stood.

The Spring Valley cemetery's oldest graves dated back to the Revolutionary War. Alone, she slowly walked the strategically laid out path between the headstones—architectural markers of life and death—imagining the days when families would bring picnic baskets, enjoying time with the living and remembering the dead. The haunting song of the Eastern Whip-poor-will called out as the birds foraged during the night. She recalled the folklore considering the singing of these birds as a death omen, that they can sense a person's soul departing and seize it as it leaves. Her grandmother called them "soul snatchers." Ada wondered what soul was caught tonight or if the birds were only capturing insects.

As she meandered through the graveyard, a gentle evening breeze rustled the leaves. Ada admired the funerary motif symbols carved in marble, each signifying a passage of life. She ran her fingers over the outline of a harvest wheat carving which symbolized a productive and significant life. The smaller makers assigned to children held an image of a flower with a broken stem symbolizing the fragility of a life cut short. An image of an up-turned boat, oar, hat, and two hands reaching out of the water honored a Navy man drowned in a boating accident.

From the corner of her eye, she detected a shadowy figure and felt a cold chill run up her spine as she walked past the mysterious mass grave of townspeople who'd died of cholera in 1873. She recalled ghost stories that echoed from the past and wondered if she'd caught a glimpse of a wandering soul. The path continued toward the southeastern portion of the cemetery —a narrow strip appropriated to the African American population—her people. A history of slaves and segregation. There were no fancy headstones for the resting place of slaves and free blacks—her slave ancestors came with the early settlers who settled in the foothills of the Appalachian Mountains and existed and worked side by side in life. In death, they were separated by a ditch with trees and bushes. She surveyed the dozens of graves of elusive dreams. Nonetheless, she thought, they'd dreamed.

With reminders of death all around her, she stood on hallowed ground. A peaceful feeling overwhelmed her as if she could step forward into eternity. Void of fear, in that very moment, she took a step, but suddenly her husband appeared, grabbed her, and pulled her back from eternity.

You're not ready. Did she hear J.R. speak those words, or did she just imagine the voice?

"I'm ready. You just have to let me go," Ada begged.

In love and fear, J.R. clasped her wrist, never loosening his death grip on his beloved.

Gasping for air, Ada woke herself. She could barely breathe, drenched in a cold sweat and shaking from the dream. She reached the other side of the bed for her husband. He wasn't there. Then she remembered she'd decided to skip church and sleep in. It was only a dream, but it seemed so real. She rubbed her arthritic wrist that held the sensation of pressure.

She fell back on her pillow, wondering why she'd dreamed of death. She and J.R. had walked through the cemetery dozens of times honoring those who'd gone before and the lives they'd forged in Spring Valley. As they stood over the graves, they always took time to reflect on their own lives. Surely, she thought, there were rational reasons for her dream. Since the pandemic, Ada had been working herself to exhaustion, all the while J.R. begging her to slow her pace. Was this a warning from beyond? Was she headed toward an early grave of unfulfilled dreams? Maybe her husband was right, and she needed to let go of one of her *pet projects*.

She was wide awake now. It was almost ten o'clock. She couldn't remember the last time she'd slept that late. She threw the covers back and slid into her house slippers. She needed one last cup of strong coffee before she switched to decaf. The launch for the Giving Tree project was only eight hours away, and she still had a few tasks to accomplish. For now, she'd let the dream stay in the land of nod.

***

She wore a new dress. Not because she wanted to celebrate the Giving Tree launch event, but because she could barely squeeze into her clothes that were now pushed to the back of the closet, hanging around and waiting for the diet to kick in. Months ago, Ada promised herself that she'd lose those pandemic pounds before the New Year. She only had five weeks before January rolled around. In all reality, she broke her promise. Her body wasn't cooperating and headed in the opposite direction. She was bloated with the extra weight gain and swelling in her stomach, ankles, and legs. She felt like she'd qualify for a Macy's Day Balloon.

Standing on the stage, Ada looked around the interior of the Mockingbird Coffee House for a final inspection. She was glad that she'd decided to move the Giving Tree onto the main floor. Partly because she needed the extra space for the volunteer event, and partly because she tried to avoid the staircase. Every time she went up and down the stairs that led to the balcony, she'd felt as if she'd run a marathon, not that she'd ever even attempted one. She just imagined how she'd feel if she did.

Especially during Christmas, Ada loved that her coffee shop was festively decorated and housed in a beautiful, historic church building with its soaring Gothic architecture. She also loved it when her customers said they felt like they'd been to church while visiting the coffee house. It was her blessed sanctuary.

To take a little bit of the hassle out of the holidays, Ada splurged and hired Abby and her professional decorating crew from the Old Towne Christmas Shop to decorate inside and out. She gave them free reign to let their creative juices flow, and that's exactly what they did, adorning the old church with festive wreaths, green winter garland, and dramatic red and white poinsettias. Below the vividly colored stained-glass, arched windows, with their illustrative portrayal of Bible stories, a beautiful addition of hand-carved, wooden nativity sets highlighting folk art styles were displayed on the window sills, nestled in pine swag with red holly berries. Ada found it awe-inspiring.

Ada checked the final task off her to-do list. It was five o'clock. She had enough time to grab a snack in the kitchen, sit down, put her feet up, and relax before the event. She wanted to slip her shoes off, but she knew from the looks of her bulging ankles that she might not get them back on, so she settled for elevating them on a chair seat. It felt so good to get off her feet. She found herself more determined than ever to consult her doctor over the painful, consistent swelling. She couldn't ignore it any longer, so she'd call and make an appointment in the morning.

***

She awoke when she heard her name, but slowly. J.R. was standing over her repeating her name. For a moment, she wasn't sure where she was until she recognized the familiar kitchen of the coffee house.

"Ada, sweetie, are you okay?"

"I must have dozed off." She willed her eyes open.

"I've been calling your cell phone for over an hour. I was getting worried," he scolded her. "The dulcimer players arrived. They're setting up on the stage." He handed her a cup of coffee. "Maybe this will help."

"Thanks, honey." She reached out for the cup as she put her feet on the floor. "I didn't mean to worry you. I was just relaxing. It was so quiet and peaceful; I just shut my eyes for a few minutes."

He bent down and kissed her forehead and took a seat across from her at the table. "Your fatigue is worrisome. I think you really need to get in and see the doctor."

"I promise I'll call and make an appointment in the morning."

"I'm going to hold you to that promise." He raised his eyebrows with that *you better keep your promise* look. "You're not a spring chicken anymore."

She might have laughed if she wasn't so darn tired. "Look who's calling the kettle black. You're no spring chicken yourself."

"Need I remind you that I passed my annual physical with flying colors. As a matter of fact, last week when I asked for the senior discount at the grocery store, the clerk didn't believe me and asked for my I.D." He beamed with pride.

"Let me tell you, it's hard living with a sexy old man who thinks he's Denzel Washington." She picked up her coffee, sipped the last drop, and slyly grinned. "But it's a burden I'll gladly bear." She stood; her throbbing ankles let her know they were still there.

J.R. rose and reached for Ada to help her steady her feet. He drew her close for a passionate kiss.

Her heart skipped a beat. As their lips parted, she caught her breath. "Wow, Denzel, what was that for?"

He laughed at her calling him Denzel. "Just because you're the love of my life."

She could hear voices and the sweet dulcimer music playing carols echoing from her sanctuary. "We'll pick up where we left off later tonight." She gave him a quick peck on his lips and headed out the door. J.R. followed and started greeting friends and neighbors.

Ada stepped on the stage and glanced around at the throngs of volunteers crowded into the coffee house, all willing to sponsor a wishing ornament from the Giving Tree, granting wishes and help to provide assistance to struggling families in need. Witnessing the overwhelming response from her Spring Valley community, it was hard for her to not burst out in tears. Before she began to speak, she eyed Blake and Courtney cuddled up closely together at a table. A smile spread across her face as she whispered a little prayer, *Thank you, Lord. Looks like our matchmaking mission is moving right along.*

Ada picked up the microphone. "Bless your hearts! What an incredible crowd. Our little town never ceases to amaze me. Thank you so much for your generous spirit."

The crowd broke out in applause.

"If you're a seasoned volunteer for the Giving Tree, bear with me because I'm going to repeat myself with a special reminder from the scriptures.

She began reading Isaiah 58:9-12: *If you get rid of unfair practices, quit blaming victims, quit gossiping about other people's sons, if you are generous with the hungry and start giving yourselves to the down-and-out, your lives will begin to glow in the darkness, your shadowed lives will be bathed in sunlight. I will always show you where to go. I'll give you a full life in the emptiest of places — firm muscles, strong bones. You will be like a well-watered garden, a gurgling spring that never runs dry. You'll use the old rubble of past lives to build a new, rebuild the foundations from out of your past. You'll be known as those who can fix anything, restore old ruins, rebuild and renovate, make the community livable again.*

The crowd sat in silent reverence as she continued.

"The spring that lies a few blocks over from this building led to the settlement of our town, Spring Valley. It has never run dry and has generously provided a life-giving water source for generations." Ada felt a cold sweat forming on her brow. She thought of how this was where she would normally get to preaching, but she felt fatigue as her speech slowed. "Our townspeople are known for having a heart of generosity. Many of you have been a recipient of their open hands. This tree and all of these ornaments of hope represent people who, just like the scripture reads, are hungry and down-and-out, needing hope for the future." She pointed to the tree branches bending from the weight of the ornaments and wishes. Her speech began to break. "Tonight, you… you will glow in the darkness as you begin…your… your quest to fulfill these Christmas wishes." She felt dizzy, swayed backwards, clutched her chest, and fell to the ground. Everyone gasped.

Blake turned to Courtney and instructed,

"Call 911. She's having a heart attack." He rushed to the stage and began administering CPR.

Ada hovered over the sanctuary. She could see Blake and could feel him compressing her chest. She saw J.R. beside her and heard him repeating her name. Panic overwhelmed her, but when she heard people in the audience praying for her, the pain in her chest and fear went away. She saw the EMTs burst through the entrance door and run to the stage.

Did she really hear her name, the prayers, or was this just another dream? If it was a dream, she thought, it seemed too real. She was cold. She closed her eyes as a feeling of peace rushed over her.

Chapter Fifteen

One of the delivery staff from the hospital's gift shop entered Ada's room and placed another floral arrangement beside her bed.

"You must be someone really important. I don't think I've ever seen so many flowers in a room," the young girl gushed over the beautiful arrangements.

"Aren't you a pretty little thing," Ada managed a smile. "I'm nobody. Just a coffee shop owner in Spring Valley."

She might fool a stranger, but J.R. knew the truth. Ada was special. To J.R. Ada was a somebody. She was—IS—his everything. It terrified him that his wife was one heartbeat away from leaving this earth. Leaving him alone.

As a pastor, he'd sat by dozens, if not hundreds, of bedsides, comforting and praying for the sick, but nothing prepared him for sitting by his wife's hospital bed, begging God for healing.

In his weakness, he prayed for strength. Strength to hold on to hope. Strength to care for his wife. Strength to withstand the financial demands that he knew would arrive in the mail. He didn't have a choice; he had to be strong for Ada. She'd been his rock during the darkest period as he ministered to parishioners during the pandemic. She'd gently pulled him out of the depths of depression and back to the land of the living.

He knew she was considered one of Spring Valley's treasures. As First Lady at AME Zion Church, she'd been ministering faithfully by his side for over four decades. Before she retired from the school system, she'd taught every first grader in town. Customers at the coffee house didn't just drop in for a cup of coffee; they came for Ada's advice. Many considered her the local therapist. The Giving Tree project she started inspired a movement of generosity in Spring Valley and forever changed the way they celebrated Christmas in their little community. Four years ago, she brought a dream to reality when she launched the local women's shelter, Haven House. Spring Valley was a better place because of Ada.

J.R. shook his head, puzzled by how she'd managed to keep all the plates spinning. It was no wonder her heart failed because she'd poured it out to everyone in the community. The needs of Spring Valley always came first.

"For heaven's sake, J.R., my room is starting to look like a funeral parlor." In a weak voice, she began barking out orders, which ordinarily, he didn't care for, but today, it made him feel somewhat relieved. "Check with the nurse's station and see what patient hasn't had any flowers delivered and send some their way."

J.R. reached for her hand and gently patted. "Stop trying to run the world, woman. You came close to sleeping in a coffin instead of your hospital bed."

"I know, I know, but—"

"Just a minute, honey. Let me stop you right there." He'd never ordered Ada around, but he had to put his foot down. "There are no ifs, ands, or buts about it. You need to stop being so worrisome and start resting. Your body needs to heal."

"Will you at least do one thing for me?"

"Depends on what it is."

"Would you text Courtney and Blake and have them drop by? I want to thank him, in person, for saving my life."

"I will," he agreed. "But don't think that I don't know what you're doing. You're still playing matchmaker from your hospital bed."

Ada shrugged her shoulders and in a weakened, feeble voice self-confessed, "Can't miss an opportunity. It's the magic of Christmas when love is in the air."

J.R. shook his head as he texted Courtney.

"How did you know that Blake administered CPR? You were out cold."

"You'll think I'm crazy, but I hovered over the sanctuary and saw and heard everything."

"Okay, if you saw everything, where was I during all the commotion?" He challenged her in disbelief.

"You were kneeling by my side, calling out my name."

His eyes widened. "So, you're telling me you had an out-of-body experience?"

"That's not all I had. At first, I was panic stricken, but when I heard the audience praying for me, my soul felt at peace. I closed my eyes and floated in a ray of light. It was beautiful. Then during my heavenly sojourn, I remember seeing my grandmother. We hugged, and she said she loved me, but I couldn't stay that I needed to return to you." Ada had an angelic glow to her face as tears welled in her eyes. "That was the last thing I remembered, until I woke up in this room with all these monitors attached to my body."

Now, he was really concerned. Since she had a glimpse of heaven where her beloved grandmother said her job wasn't finished on earth, he feared she'd work warp speed instead of slowing down.

His phone vibrated, alerting him to a text. "Courtney and Blake will stop by after their shift on the Health Bus. She said they'd already planned on visiting."

Ada could barely keep her eyes open. "I think I'll take a little nap until they arrive. Love you."

She was in deep sleep most of the afternoon. J.R. stayed by her side.

***

Ada opened her eyes and saw her husband napping

in the recliner next to her hospital bed. She surveyed the room. The walls were a calming, comforting light blue, trimmed in sterile white. Vertical blinds were partially open, allowing access to the mountain view and letting daylight spill into the room. The delicate, sweet aroma of peonies filled the room with the cheeriness of a sun-soaked spring day.

Anxious, Ada examined the monitors hooked to her body. She'd watched countless TV episodes of medical shows to know the monitor connected to the electrodes and wires was an electrocardiogram recording the continuous electrical activity of her heart. The nasal prongs, while annoying, delivered much needed oxygen. Attached to her index finger was a clip-like devise measuring oxygen levels. She knew there was no way around getting out of bed and use the toilet without assistance from hospital staff. She lay in bed dreading what the future held.

J.R. was suddenly awoken by a quick jerk, as if to catch himself from falling. He'd only been able to sleep in snatches. He found Ada staring at the ceiling. "I'm sorry. I must have dozed off. I didn't realize you were awake."

"I just woke up a few minutes ago, and I didn't want to disturb you. You look so tired." Ada was concerned over his lack of sleep. They both couldn't be laid up. "Is the recliner comfortable?"

"Actually, it's quite cozy. The nurse brought me a pillow and blanket, and I snuggled up last night and got a few winks in." He brought the recliner back into an upright position and looked at the clock on the wall. "The doctor should be here in the next few minutes. They said to expect him between four and five this afternoon."

"Can't wait," Ada murmured under her breath.

"Let's look on the bright side. Hopefully, he has some good news."

"I could use a little good news about now," Ada struggled with a smile. There was so much to worry about. So many responsibilities. Commitments. Obligations. Who would carry the load? A favorite hymn, inspired from a scripture, interrupted her thoughts: *His eye is on the sparrow, and I know He watches me.* She decided it was a reminder to practice what she preached. She knew, without a shadow of a doubt, that God would provide for whatever she needed. She remembered the scripture. *Which of you by being anxious can add a single hour to his span of life?* Today, she thought, no matter what the future held, worry would hold no power over her.

She whispered, "Thank you, Jesus, for another day."

She heard a gentle tap on the door. Courtney poked her head in to see if Ada was alert. "Anybody home?"

Ada motioned for Courtney and Blake to come in. J.R. stood to shake Blake's hand and gave Courtney a big hug before she went to Ada's bedside. They were both still dressed in their scrubs.

"You two are a sight for sore eyes. I'm so glad you stopped in. I wanted to thank Blake, in person, for saving my life. You were truly a God-send."

Blake patted her hand. "I'm just thankful I was there when you needed me."

"You and me both," Ada managed to smile. "How's everything working out on the Health Bus?" She was interested, but she really wanted to ask how things were going in the romance department. She'd wait and ask Courtney in private.

"It's quite the adventure. I didn't know what to expect when they asked me to fill in, but I'm enjoying it." Courtney looked over at Blake for affirmation.

"There are definitely challenges, but the reward of serving the medically under-served is gratifying. Honestly, I didn't realize the overwhelming need in the area. It's been eye-opening, to say the least. Every day we finish, I feel like we made a difference."

Ada loved that he used 'we' including himself and Courtney. She considered *we* a promising pronoun. She took that as a cue to let go and let God take over matchmaking. "I'm proud of you two making such an impact in our little community."

"Ada, I know you're lying in this bed worrying about all your obligations. But that should be the farthest thing from your mind," Courtney assured her. "You know how organized Shauna is, and she's already arranged for someone to take over the Giving Tree project. Your assistant manager has stepped up and will take over the coffee house responsibilities until you're healthy enough to take back the reigns. We just want you to concentrate on recovery."

"Amen to that!" J.R. chimed in, "You've taken a great load off of our shoulders."

Before Ada could object, a young man in a white coat with a stethoscope draped around his neck, clasping an iPad entered the room. Stands of gray weaved in his dark brown hair. Ada guessed it wasn't due to his age because he was a young pup. She knew all too well that stress had a way of prematurely accelerating graying. He made his introductions and stood at the foot of Ada's bed.

"We'll scoot out and let you have time with your doctor," Blake announced.

Ada noticed that he gently put his hand on the small of Courtney's back to guide her to the door. It thrilled her heart to witness the protective, romantic gesture. "God bless you two! Thank you for the visit."

Courtney turned and formed a heart with her hands. Ada knew she was loved.

"Okay, young man. What's the damage?" Ada got straight to the point.

"First, Mrs. Taylor, I'm encouraged by your improvement in the past twenty-four hours. I know you feel scared, confused, and overwhelmed. That's a natural response. The paramedics had to shock and stabilize you en route to the hospital. When you collapsed, you went into cardiac arrest and had a large heart attack with additional clots forming. We performed an emergency angioplasty to open up the arteries. You'll probably be with us for about a week, and depending on how well you rehab, you may not be able to return to work full time for two to three months." He watched as her eyes glazed over trying to take it all in. "I hear you own a coffee shop and have the best desserts in town."

"I don't like to brag, but I'm known for my Hummingbird Cake. Do you think we could barter my hospital bill with desserts?" She forced a smile.

He grinned. "I don't think the hospital billing department would go for that."

Ada closed her eyes for a moment and took a deep breath when the doctor paused.

"Our job—and your job—is to lower the risk of another heart attack. You'll need to change pre-heart attack habits."

Ada hoped that J.R. was listening closely as she became overwhelmed with his instructions. In her foggy brain, she boiled it down to take medications, keep follow-up appointments, increase physical activity, begin a heart-healthy diet, and accept support from family and friends. She vaguely remembered something about wearing a portable electrocardiogram once she was released from the hospital. She nodded her head up and down in acknowledgement. She hadn't fully accepted the challenges and the new life changes he'd described, but she would. She knew her life depended upon it.

Chapter Sixteen

Blake found practicing medicine on the Health Bus more challenging than normal hours in a clinic. He'd spent the past week treating the normal stream of patients with acute disease management, diabetes, flu vaccines, and an outbreak of strep throat. He'd lost count of the tongue depressors he'd used. After three days of appointments on the bus, on Thursday and Friday he completed paperwork at the hospital. He also visited the Human Resource department to declare he and Courtney were officially dating. HR frowned on the situation, but it wasn't forbidden. He was forewarned of the potential downfalls which he was more familiar with than he wanted to be. Hopefully, this relationship would have a happier outcome. When he wasn't working side-by-side with Courtney in the bus, he wished he was.

He spent a leisurely Saturday morning, starting with his workout, a quick shower, and Chef Jean's gourmet breakfast. He'd looked forward to the coastal breakfast skillet she had on the menu board, and it did not disappoint. The hearty meal was served in a personal-sized cast iron skillet and filled with chopped bacon, diced red potatoes, peeled shrimp, onion, grape tomatoes, scrambled eggs, cheddar cheese, and chopped avocado. The dish tasted like breakfast at his favorite diner in the Outer Banks.

While he dined, Blake watched guests from across the dining room and found himself thinking of his granddad. He remembered how he felt the last time they'd sat on the front porch, staring at the ocean and reminiscing. They had spent the afternoon chatting and laughing about his childhood sailing trips when Granddad made him feel so grown up and important when he let Blake serve as his first mate. Blake hoped that wasn't their last conversation—he feared it may have been. He didn't take a selfie that day, but the scene was etched in his memory.

While his thoughts floated back in time, Blake's eyes landed on an older gentleman sitting near him in the dining room. The family of multiple generations surrounded the grandfatherly man, and Blake's stomach received a pang of loneliness from sitting on the outside of such an intimate moment for them. Blake felt compelled to honor the scene in front of him.

He grabbed a child's paper placemat. On the blank side, he sketched a drawing of the old man with his toddler grandchild sitting on his lap. They sat in a wingback chair, next to the fireplace that warmed the room, and a decorated tree stood adjacent to the chair. His wrinkly hands held a book that monopolized their time while the rest of the family finished breakfast. In a Norman Rockwell fashion, Blake captured a moment of emotional bonding in everyday life. His grandmother always said he had a special gift. He gave the drawing to the elderly man as he left, and the man held it in his trembling hand in awe of the intricate sketch.

Blake looked forward to the afternoon, sharing a holiday tradition with Courtney and her children. It wasn't like any traditional first date he'd experienced. This would be the first for him to include a couple of kiddos. But it didn't matter to him. Maybe he'd have his own Rockwellish, emotional-bonding moment as they cut and trimmed a tree together.

Blake exited the inn's parking lot, turned down Main Street, and followed the soothing voice of the GPS girl that guided his path. Out of curiosity, once he'd Googled her and discovered the face behind the voice was beautiful and blonde. As he scrolled through her pictures, he decided he'd follow her anywhere, even when she drove him crazy and once calmy almost propelled him off a cliff with her haywire directions. He could silence her voice, but he didn't—they had this weird connection. She kept him company on lonely trips. They'd traveled so many miles together—he just couldn't let her go.

As planned, Blake arrived at one-thirty in the afternoon. After the thirty-minute drive, the golden voice informed him, "You've reached your final destination."

Carefully navigating this unfamiliar territory with Courtney, Blake wondered if their relationship would be their final destination.

He scolded himself, *One day at a time, buddy; don't move too fast. It may be a dead-end.*

From the kitchen window, Courtney saw him park the Jeep. Before he had a chance to get out of the vehicle, she opened the door and waved him inside. The GPS girl was instantly erased from his memory. The beautiful brunette standing on the porch was all he had on his mind.

When Blake walked in, the corgi happily rushed to greet their guest.

"You've already met Nick." She gestured to the jumping dog. "Hope you like him because he'll follow you everywhere."

Nick was cuteness overload. Blake wasn't personally familiar with the stubby little breed, but he was well-informed enough on popular culture to know that they were included in the royal family as Queen Elizabeth adored the corgis that were her constant companions.

Chance and Gracie appeared from their rooms to investigate the commotion. Not fully dressed for their adventure, Courtney warned the kids, "Smells like it's going to snow, so you need extra layers. Go back and dig out your caps, scarves, and gloves." Their expressions told her they had no desire to bundle up.

Blake looked at her like she was from a

different planet. "You smelled snow?"

"Yes, when I stepped outside this morning and took a whiff of the air, I smelled snow."

"You smelled snow?" he repeated, doubting her forecast.

She had a suspicious feeling he was mocking her. "Haven't you ever smelled snow? I don't know how to explain it. There's a cold, fresh scent in the air."

He cocked his head and raised his eyebrow.

"Mark my word, ice crystals are forming as we speak."

After Courtney made sure the kids were covered from head to toe, Blake, with chain saw in hand, smiled thinking they resembled a scene from *National Lampoon's Christmas Vacation* on the hunt for the perfect tree. On the track to the mountain, they walked past Rich's garage.

Rich called out when he saw them, "I see your tree hunting quest." Rich knew of their plans, and he intended to be the lumberjack. But Alana, the matchmaker, insisted that he stay home and let Blake take his place. When Blake got a peek of Rich's car collection through the open door, he started to walk toward the garage. The kids followed. Courtney stood her ground, hoping they would turn around and stay on task. They kept walking. She followed.

The candy-apple red, restored 1940 Ford pickup first caught Blake's eye. He ran his hand over the curved, flowing body lines. "This is incredible." He didn't say out loud, but he thought it was the perfect transportation for Santa.

"I call her Betsy," Rich introduced. "She was a member of our family before I was born."

Blake was like a kid in a candy shop admiring the collection. He could imagine himself cruising along the beach in Rich's 1963 Sting Ray, split-window Corvette.

"Remember, Dad spent his career in NASCAR. Needless to say, he likes fast cars." Courtney glanced over and smiled at her dad.

Blake eyed Chance walking toward the custom black and white checkered flag designed cornhole boards with red and green bags. They appeared to be in the correct position, twenty-seven feet from the front edge to front edge of the boards. "Looks like somebody likes to play cornhole."

Courtney wished he hadn't noticed. This was going to delay their tree cutting.

***

Chance begged to play a quick game. As soon as his papaw had them agree to an abbreviated set, Chance, lickety-split chose Gracie as his partner. Courtney volunteered to sit this one out as Rich and Gabe teamed up against the kids. Gabe thought they would easily edge out the competition.

Teasing, Gabe proceeded with some smack talk. "I'm considered a champion at my favorite bar and grill back home. The last time I won, we played on the beach under a full moon. So, under these pristine conditions, you'll probably be handing me a trophy."

Puzzled, Gracie looked at her mother. "Mom, what does pristy mean?"

Courtney slowly pronounced, "It's pristine. It means everything is perfectly set up for cornhole. The floor is even, and there's no wind or sun beating down on us. It's the ideal setting for the game."

"That doesn't matter to me and Chance. We can play anywhere," Gracie innocently explained.

Anticipating the outcome, Rich looked over at his sweet granddaughter and winked.

Chance proved hard, if not impossible, to beat. Blake learned firsthand they were a competitive family; even little Gracie had a cutthroat streak. Being the baby boy with three much older sisters, Blake always somehow managed to win the battles. Video games, board games, beach bowling, or collecting the most seashells—it didn't matter, they always let Blake win. They were his personal cheerleading squad. He loved his sisters, but also blamed his sisters for his inflated sense of ego. They would say they just didn't want to see him sad and disappointed.

They alternated pitching bags until it came down to the last toss.

Chance stood in the designated pitcher's box and proceeded to pitch the most difficult rolling shot through the board hole. He jumped up and down like bouncing on a trampoline. "We walloped you!"

Shocked that he was crushed by two juveniles, Blake turned on his partner. "You knew, didn't you?"

Rich's eyes twinkled. "Just sayin', they're a couple of backyard hustlers. Players beware."

"I was bamboozled by a couple of bambinos." Blake jokingly pointed his index finger at the pair. "I challenge you to another game. Next time, I won't go easy on you."

"Nyah nyah nyah nyah nyah," Gracie taunted Blake in a sing-song voice, accompanied by sticking out her tongue.

"Grace Lily Clarke, you know better than that," Courtney scolded.

Gracie knew she was in big trouble when her mom used her full name. She didn't think it necessary to apologize because it was just a joke, but she wanted to please her mom. In a flash, Gracie bounced over to Blake. She gave him her puppy-dog look. "I'm sorry, Mr. Blake."

Blake scooped her up and gave Gracie a big hug. "That's okay, we were just having some fun."

As soon as her feet touched the ground, she turned to Rich with the same adorable expression. "Papaw, can we have a pop?"

As usual, Rich fixed eyes on Courtney for final approval. When she nodded, Rich dug change from his pocket to feed the machine. Still in a competitive mode, Chance and Gracie raced to raid the coke machine, leaving Blake and Courtney behind.

The vintage Coca Cola machine was iconic red with white rounded tops and "Iced Cold" written on the bottom in white lettering. Rich had been offered a lot of money for the Holy Grail of vending machines, especially after he had it restored, but he'd turn them down. Nostalgia wouldn't allow him to part with the vending machine—it was part of his childhood. As long as Rich could remember, it held a prominent place in his dad's Auto Shop. It came with the building when his dad opened his shop. Rich remembered dropping coins in the slot as he waited for the chilled glass bottle to drop, so he could quench his thirst. Sometimes he would press the cold bottle to his temple to cool his brow from the sultry heat. To Rich, it was priceless. A cherished memory. He handed Chance and Gracie coins, and the tradition continued.

"Gulp it down quick. We need to find a tree," Courtney rushed the kids along.

The last two Christmases, Courtney worked hard to make them special since her children's lives had been so stressful. One of the family's new favorite holiday traditions was the hunt for the Christmas tree on the farm. Part of their "cut-your-own" experience included the hike. But when the morning air filled with snow flurries, Rich encouraged them to take his Gator utility vehicle.

Girls in the front seat and guys in the back,

Courtney sped toward the mountain that rose up in their back pasture. Passengers were holding on for dear life. "I take it you like fast cars, too!" Blake yelled from the back. Courtney answered by pushing harder on the gas. The kids loved it.

They enjoyed the hunt but set a record on how fast they chose a tree—more due to the weather than picking the perfect Balsam. By the time they returned and parked in her front yard with their treasure, the snow dusting turned to over an inch of accumulation. Blake and Courtney untied the ropes and wrestled with the tree as the kids played in the snow.

"Let's make our first snowman." Gracie started rolling a ball of snow.

Ever the planner, when Courtney smelled the snow in the air, she took a tarp to drape over the tree. A little moisture had still gathered, but it would dry in a few hours while she cooked, and they dined.

While the kids built their snowpal, Courtney invited Blake inside to help with dinner.

Chapter Seventeen

She moved around the kitchen like a professional, he thought, as Courtney pulled the vegetables from the refrigerator, grabbed a knife and cutting board and began slicing vegetables at break neck speed.

"Seriously, you've got some culinary skills."

"I picked up a lot of pro tips working at a diner in high school, and I've helped Chef Jean out at the inn from time to time." She knew her life story wasn't as glamour and heroic as his, but it was her story. "It's proven to come in handy with the kids. Most days I feel like a short-order cook."

She dumped the green peppers and onions in the frying pan. The oil sizzled. "By the way, we're having burritos. Is that okay with you?"

"Perfect. I could live on Taco Bell."

She smiled as if challenged. "Oh, I guarantee this will put to shame Taco Bell."

She added another pan to the stove, adjusted the flame, and began browning the meat. She pointed to the pantry Blake was leaning against. "Would you grab the tortillas, salsa, and chips?"

He took the items and placed them on the countertop. He ripped open the bag and munched on a chip.

She placed a bowl on the countertop. "Go ahead and open the salsa for your chips."

"I bet you meet a lot of interesting people on your medical assignments," Courtney opened the conversation. Her back was to him for a moment until he walked over beside the stove and leaned with his back toward the counter, so he could see her face.

"None as interesting as you." He slowly tucked a string of hair behind her ear.

The tender moment didn't go unnoticed. Courtney kept an eye on the skillet all the while glancing at Blake as she leaned toward him anticipating a kiss. Their lips met.

What sounded like a bucking rodeo bull charged up the porch steps. Interrupted, Courtney and Blake looked over to see the kids with the dog in tow racing through the front entrance.

In unison they announced, "We made a snowman! Come look."

Gracie held the door open to show off their tilting snow sculpture in the front yard.

"I love it!"

"I'm impressed!" Blake agreed.

"He's not as big as we wanted, but we needed a bigger snowfall." Chance followed the motto, the bigger the better.

"Okay, that's enough. You're letting the cold in." Courtney started to close the door.

Gracie stuck her head out and yelled, "Happy Birthday!

"It's not my birthday." Blake teased Gracie.

"I know, silly, it's Frosty's birthday!"

"Gracie, after dinner, you can show Blake your Frosty the Snowman book. It's been a long time since he was a little guy, and it sounds like he's forgotten the happy birthday part of the book."

After Joshua's funeral, his mother packed a box full of the kids' books and toys. The kind gesture gave them remnants of the life they'd had with their father. Gracie was thrilled to discover her treasured little book, *Frosty the Snowman*. She was obsessed with Frosty when she was a toddler. It became the most requested book for her dad's bedtime story time.

"From the looks of you two, I think you rolled in the snow a few times." She gave them that *what in the world have you been up to* look. "Go put on some dry clothes. By the time you're finished changing, supper will be on the table."

Gracie slipped out of her coat and boots and made a mad dash to her bedroom, leaving Chance behind. Seeking warmth, the dog curled up in front of the fireplace.

Chance saw the chips and salsa on the counter. "Yeah! It's burrito night." He sat on the floor and struggled with his snow boots.

"Here, let me help, little guy." Blake stood over Chance. "Give me your foot." With one yank, the first boot was off. In a matter of seconds, the second foot was free. Chance's feet were like ice.

"When you change and put on clean socks, come back and sit by the fireplace with Nick and warm up your toes."

Courtney's heart melted as she watched Blake with her children. He was born to be a father, she thought. She just didn't know if God had plans for him to be a father to her children. She had a lot of questions for her Heavenly Father. Sometimes her plans were not His plans.

The table was set with disposable, tree-shaped plates, themed with the Nutcracker characters of the Sugarplum Fairy, the Mouse King, and the Nutcracker toy that came to life. It made for an easy cleanup and set a festive mood. The dinner conversation was lively, especially when Blake told stories of working on the Mercy Ship, a hospital ship in South Africa and how they avoided piracy at sea. They peppered Blake with questions about his adventures as they munched on their burritos. His storytelling had them hooked at pirate ships. She knew they pictured Johnny Depp as Captain Sparrow in *Pirates of the Caribbean*, not the modern-day pirates the Mercy Ship avoided. Gracie already thought Blake hung the moon. It took Chance a little longer to warm up to him, but the pirate story bonded them for life.

"If we're going to trim the tree, we need to get on it." Courtney started cleaning off the table as the kids hurried toward the tree. She started to brew a fresh pot of coffee but remembered hot cocoa was on the menu for the evening's activities.

She'd solider on without her drink of choice.

Positioned as the focal point of the room, the tree stood naked in front of the family room window waiting to be dressed, merry and bright. The smell of fresh-cut pine permeated the room, putting everyone in a joyous mood.

"Should we call Papaw and Nana Alana to see if they want to help?" Gracie loved her papaw and nana and wanted to include him in everything.

"I asked them earlier, and they already had plans for the evening, but they're going to stop by tomorrow to see your masterpiece and bring presents to put under the tree."

Gracie clapped with anticipation as Chance started opening boxes of decorations they'd retrieved from storage. He was a little sad they didn't have any ornaments from his old house, but he was old enough to know that when they left home and moved into the shelter, they left everything behind. His old life seemed so long ago. He liked his new life. His room. His papaw and Alana. He even was starting to like Blake.

Gracie ran to her bedroom to retrieve her favorite ornament. Two Christmases ago at the Santa Depot, she'd whispered her wish in Santa's ear and to her amazement, somehow, Santa delivered. She wished they could move from the shelter to a house of their own and that she would have a princess bedroom she didn't have to share. After their photo session, Santa gave Gracie and Chance an ornament depicting Santa kneeling at the nativity with baby Jesus. She kept the special ornament on her bookshelf all year long to remember her wish that came true.

As Gracie finished hanging her Santa ornament, she realized another item was missing. "Mommy, we forgot Teddy." Gracie ran down the hallway.

A few seconds later she yelled, "Mommy, I can't reach him."

Courtney sat on the floor wresting with a strand of tangled lights. She looked at Blake and asked for help.

"No problem. I'll go."

Blake followed the noise and found Gracie in her mother's bedroom, standing on her tippy toes with arms stretched toward a stuffed toy bear sitting high on top of a tall chest of drawers.

"I've almost got it."

Blake grinned. He liked her determination, but she wasn't even close. "I'll give you a boost."

He picked Gracie up by her waist and lifted her high enough to grab the bear.

As soon as her feet touched the ground, she took off running back toward the family room.

"No running in the house." If Courtney had said it once, she'd said it a thousand times.

As he walked behind Gracie toward the family room, Blake caught himself staring at the amazing woman still sitting in the middle of the floor on the verge of winning the battle with the tangled tree lights. In her countdown to

Christmas, she was making the house feel festive and cozy, creating happy, magical memories for Chance and Gracie—even for him.

He hadn't planned for this. He'd planned to spend three months in Spring Valley and move on. Then Courtney happened. Now, his heart was leading him to follow a different path. He reminded himself that he'd followed that path before—the path to a broken heart.

Courtney could feel his eyes on her. She glanced up. When their eyes met, she smiled.

She took his breath away. It was a contented smile—full of genuine happiness. Warmth filled his chest. His heart leaped, reminding Blake that his heart had healed.

Maybe, he considered, he should let go of fear and let love lead his path. Love—was he in love?

Blake watched as Gracie placed the toy bear on the patchwork-quilted tree skirt. Angel, the cat, wearing red tinsel garland around her fury little neck, snuggled up next to the stuffed bear like an old friend. Chance held a strand of colored lights, fixated on perfect placement as he went round and round the tree stringing the lights.

Gracie made introductions, "Blake, that's Teddy, Mommy's Christmas bear."

"Teddy's seen better days. Looks like he's been around for a long, long time."

"I beg your pardon," Courtney stood, hands on hips and playfully scolded Blake. "I'm not for sure if you meant to, but you just insulted your host. I don't know how old you think I am, but I've not been around a long, long, long time." Her eyes teased. "And for your information, Teddy is not worn out; he's love worn."

Blake threw his hands up in defeat. "I'm sorry. First, in my defense, it was only two long, long times. Secondly, I didn't intend to insult you or Teddy. You're both adorable."

Courtney laughed, "Keep it up. Flattery may just get you out of the doghouse."

At the mention of a dog, Nick starting barking.

"This has turned into a three-ring circus. Loud music, a bear, a talking dog, a fancy cat, and two little monkeys." Courtney added to the chaos when she tickled Gracie. Her daughter laughed uncontrollably, escaped her mother's tickles, and begged Chance to let her help with the lights.

Instead, he gave her silver icicle tinsel. Appeased, one-by-one, tinsel-by-tinsel, Gracie accessorized the tree.

Blake nodded toward the front door.

"Would you step outside with me?'

"Now? It's snowing out there."

"Just for a minute—two at the most. There are two thousand strands of tinsel in that box to keep them occupied."

Courtney watched as her kids decorated. She could stay and be the Ring Master or break away to be alone with Blake.

"Kids, we'll be right back."

The happy decorators didn't even notice they'd stepped out.

Blake smiled and took her hand as they stepped outside on the porch.

When the icy air stung her face, she wished she'd grabbed a coat. Pretending she didn't know his intentions, she looked in his eyes and asked, "Why are we outside in the cold?"

"I didn't want to do this in front of the kids."

He drew her close, ran his fingers through her hair, and cupped her face in his hands as his lips touched hers.

On this wintry night, wrapped in his arms, she felt warm, not from the heat of their closeness, but from the undeniable truth that Blake filled her life with the warmth of happiness. Locked in his embrace, thoughts swirled in her mind. *Their home had been robbed of joy, but could Blake be offering the gift of happiness?*

You overthink, she reminded herself. From the other side of the door, the volume rose from the three-ring circus. When she heard her name called out, she stepped backward.

"As much as I hate to say it, we need to go back in."

He curled his fingers around hers. His eyes begged her to stay.

"That's not fair, don't look at me that way."

As she turned and reached for the door handle, he pulled her back to him and gently kissed her forehead. Her heart melted.

It was eleven before Blake left. The kids were tucked in bed. Away from prying eyes, Blake and Courtney said their goodbyes inside, in the warmth of the house.

After he was gone, Courtney sat alone on the couch, wrapped in a cozy quilt. She could hardly wait to see Blake again. They'd planned a shopping trip Sunday afternoon while the kids were at play practice. She started counting down the hours.

The twinkling lights on the tree gave her warm fuzzies. She gave herself permission to ignore the decorating disarray. The empty holiday storage bins half-stacked in one corner. Displaced ornaments the cat knocked off a low-lying branch, scattered on the floor. She'd get to it in the morning. She just wanted to sit and think for a moment.

Spying her love-worn bear nestled under the tree, she realized she hadn't finished telling Blake about her childhood teddy bear. Courtney looked Teddy in his coal-black, button eyes and talked to her old friend, "Remind me to tell Blake your whole remarkable story." It might have been the reflection of the light, but his eyes twinkled.

Blake's goodnight kiss lingered in her thoughts. Did she kiss him because she loved that he played with her kids? Gracie didn't open up so easily to newcomers. Courtney noticed, Gracie even held his hand when she played tour guide and showed him the house. Gracie would have been too young to remember playing with her dad. Chance was five when his dad had the accident and could no longer wrestle around with his son. That was Chance's love language—he loved to wrestle. She realized he hadn't played like that with anyone for years—until today.

She kissed him because she wanted to.

She was blessed that Blake entered their lives.

Chapter Eighteen

S unday morning Courtney woke to the sound of Nick's high-pitched barking, pleading to be let out for a potty break. She had fallen asleep on the couch the night before and slept through till morning without waking in the wee hours, stumbling, like a zombie, to her own bed.

The air was chilly. She wrapped the quilt around her and hurried to let the dog out before he had an accident on her holiday entry rug. She closed the door behind him but stayed close since she knew the snow would quicken his business. While she patiently waited, she remembered it was Sunday. If they were going to make it on time for church, she and the kids needed to get moving.

The dog let out a single sharp bark, signaling he'd completed his task. She wiped his paws dry and sent him to fetch Chance.

Her body didn't wake by itself; she needed coffee. She made her way to the kitchen for her morning ritual. She spooned the ground, dark-roast coffee beans into the filter, poured fresh hot water in the reservoir, then hit the switch. She chose from her collection a decorative mug with the quote, "Life Happens—Coffee Helps." She murmured to herself, *Isn't that the truth*.

While waiting for it to brew, she warmed the cup in the microwave and added exactly one teaspoon of sugar—none of that fake stuff—and two teaspoons of half and half creamer. The same way her mother took her coffee. The morning she turned thirteen, Courtney's mom allowed her to drink coffee. She remembered feeling so grown-up. Every morning they bonded over coffee, until she was gone. In a matter of minutes, she'd be enjoying a smooth, rich cup of glorious coffee. Then her day could begin.

***

Sunday afternoon Courtney met Blake at the inn. They strolled down to the Old Towne Christmas Shop for a shopping spree. The store had a magical, shop-till-you drop Christmas wonderland feel with its rooms overflowing with twinkling lights, trimmed trees, and garland and filled with trims and unique gifts. Local crafts took center stage with hand-carved ornaments, corn shuck dolls, nativities, custom Santa dolls, quilts, and pottery. *An Appalachian Christmas* album from folk fiddler, Mark O'Connor, was playing joyous holiday songs in the background, adding to the old-time holiday atmosphere.

To Blake, it smelled like Christmas with the evergreen, spice, and sugary peppermint capturing the essence of the holiday.

The shop was located in an old building, which for many years housed a 19th century pharmacy. The vintage fixtures were marble and oak, not ornate, but simple and sturdy. The built-in oak cabinets that once held old, amber-glass medicine bottles were loaded with merchandise. Delicate, custom Santa dolls and exquisite folk-art pieces were presented behind the vintage glass display cases. From generations of foot traffic, the wear on the creaking wood floors added a yesterday charm. Along the east wall stood the marble soda fountain, a nostalgic icon where old and young found a place to gather. Now, Comet Cookie Company, a reindeer-themed cocoa and cookie shop, provided a break for shoppers sitting at the marble counters, munching on cookies and sipping hot cocoa while watching holiday movies on the flat screen behind the counter.

"I smell fresh-baked cookies. Before we leave, we have to stop at the cookie counter."

"You're as bad as the kids. As soon as we walk through the door, they make a bee line for cookies and cocoa every visit."

"Can you blame them?"

Together they wandered through the store. Blake decided to go with an ornament theme for the women in his family. For his mother, he picked up a quilted partridge and pear from the 12 Days of Christmas series. It was delicately shaped, stuffed, and handsewn.

"Good choice." Courtney smiled. "That's one of mine."

"Did you make this?"

"Yes, my hobby is quilting. Colleen added my collection to the store this year. All summer I was quilting ornaments."

"They're exquisite!" He added four more sets for his sisters and grandmothers to his shopping bag.

"That does it for me. I'm ready for a cookie."

"Are you going for a shopping speed record?" She looked in his bag to see if it held anything. "Let's mosey around for a few minutes before treats." She reached for his arm.

The touch of her fingers wrapped around his arm warmed his heart.

They strolled to the back section of the store. Courtney heard a familiar voice and quickly realized it was her friend Abby assisting another customer. They made eye contact. Abby wiggled her eyebrows up and down in approval when she saw Courtney with Blake.

Courtney gave her that *don't embarrass me* kind of look.

Puzzled why Abby wasn't at play practice, as soon as Abby finished with her customer, Courtney inquired, "What are you doing here? You should be at the theatre."

"The assistant director is handling practice today. Mom is under the weather, so I had to cover for her at the store. I'm so happy Gracie and Chance decided to join the cast. They'll love it." Abby was always recruiting potential young stars. "I won't keep you. Enjoy your shopping. Blake, it was good seeing you." She had to add, "You two look happy together."

The unexpected comment left Blake speechless. All he could come up with slipped out of his mouth, "Thank you. Merry Christmas!"

Courtney smiled as she laid her head on his shoulder and mocked him. "Thank you. Merry Christmas?" They both laughed.

"By the way, you know that Gracie and Chance are expecting you at the Christmas play, right?" That was Courtney's way of inviting Blake.

"I wouldn't miss it for the world. Text me the time and place, and I'll be there."

Courtney decided she was ready for caffeine and led the way to the Comet Cookie Company counter where she ordered coffee with a gingerbread cookie. Blake ordered hot cocoa and a half dozen sugar cookies. She looked at him in disbelief.

"What?" He shrugged his shoulders. "I told you I love sugar cookies." Blake devoured a cookie in one bite.

It was fun. Shopping with Blake, coffee, cookies, gossiping. She'd opened her heart and looked forward to celebrating the new year with Blake.

"We have about forty minutes before I need to pick up the kids. Let's start planning our Giving Tree project."

Blake agreed. He'd spend all evening with her if she allowed.

Courtney pulled out her phone and searched for the email that Shauna had sent with the names of the families living in the travel trailers on the church property. She read off the ages of the children and their Christmas wishes. "I think we should provide a gift for the parents, as well."

"That's a great idea. What do you have in mind?"

"Coffee and chocolate are always a good idea."

"Of course, you'd choose coffee. I think coffee runs through your veins."

"My mom tried to convince me that she knew the writers for the *Gilmore Girls*, and Lorelai and Rory's obsession with coffee was based on my mother and me. I naively believed her."

"My sisters never missed an episode of that show. I watched a few times, but it didn't click with me. But the way my sisters gossiped about the lives of the characters, you would have thought they lived in Stars Hallow."

"If you can recall the name of the town, I think somebody watched the *Gilmore Girls* more than he wants to admit."

"I'm not admitting to anything." He zipped his lips.

"I'll stop with one quote of Lorelai's that I live by." To emphasize the point, she held her coffee cup and spoke quickly, "Coffee, coffee, coffee!"

"You need serious help."

She stared at him over her cup. "No, what I

need is coffee, coffee, coffee."

He laughed, took another giant bite of a cookie, and suggested they get to the task at hand.

"All kidding aside, you have to admit it's a practical gift that most people would like. The Mockingbird Coffee House has their private label, and all profits from the coffee bag sales are donated to the Haven House women's shelter." She sat staring into space, calculating in her mind. "A one-pound bag serves about 32 cups, so that should last about a week."

Blake interrupted. "For you, it might last two or three days."

She knew he spoke truth. Without missing a beat, she continued, "And we could pick up chocolates at the candy store down on East Main."

"Sounds like a plan. Let's see how many gifts for the kids we can knock out at this store, and we'll be well on our way." Blake shoved in the last cookie, stood, and grabbed another shopping bag. With a mouth full, he exclaimed, "Ho, ho, ho! Let's go, go, go!"

She gulped down her coffee. "It's not a race, you know." She took another shopping bag and chased after him. The flutter in her heart didn't surprise her. She was falling in love. She couldn't help but be suspicious of Blake's heart and motives. But in this time of her life, wasn't she supposed to be suspicious of everyone? For now—she believed everything seemed right.

Chapter Nineteen

In four hundred and forty-four miles, he'd be home. It was one o'clock in the morning when he unexpectantly checked out at the inn. He called the hospital to let them know he had a family emergency. He wanted to call Courtney, but she needed her sleep. He'd contact her later. Traffic was light. Except for headlights, the highway was pitch black.

He wondered if the triple number, 444, had a significant meaning. The significance for him meant his life was about to change.

Since Blake took his first breath, his granddad had been a part of his life. Nearing death, his granddad was about to take his last breath. God would call him home. He would walk this earth no more.

When Blake last saw him in September, he knew Granddad was nearing the end. They both knew, but they didn't discuss it. Instead, they sat on the porch, a wind chime fluttering in the wind, gently playing a song of mourning. They sat listening for a while, soaking in the sun rays and memories.

They stared beyond his grandma's favorite magnolia tree and the majestic southern live oak out into the ocean, and they talked. Reliving days of sailing. Days of fishing. Just remembering the journey called life with Granddad.

Before Blake left, they embraced—the kind of embrace that meant something. The kind where neither one of them wanted to let go, but they knew they couldn't hold on forever. He recalled his granddad's parting words. *I love you, Grandson. Remember, a fish will never realize its potential until you throw it in water. Now sail into the dingbatters world, find your potential, and live your passion.*

That day, he did as he was instructed. He left the island—his granddad's world, flew to Africa, and sailed the Mercy Ship, rekindling his passion of caring for the sick.

His mind kept falling back to 444. Curious, Blake picked up his phone and asked Siri, "Siri, what do the numbers 444 mean?"

In the dark, the soft, comforting voice replied, "In numerology, 444 is considered a significant number that guides people throughout their lives. According to the Associated Press, it is 'an assurance that one is on the right path in life.' It helps clear doubts about the right direction and encourage perseverance with the current approach."

Wow! He wasn't expecting that. He may be stretching it a bit to come to a desired conclusion, but Granddad was his '444'—Blake's guiding force throughout his entire life.

He mulled over the other definition, "an assurance

that one is on the right path in life."

Was he on the right path? He felt like he was on the right path.

He re-set cruise control to a few miles over the speed limit and hoped he wouldn't get a ticket. He wanted to arrive before his granddad left.

When he passed Winston Salem, he was half-way home. He stopped to refuel his tank and load up on snacks and caffeine. He took the outer belt around Raleigh and on to State Route 64. When he hit Rocky Mount, NC, he only had two more hours. His cell phone rang. He glanced and saw his mom's face. He knew she was calling to tell him he was too late. He wasn't ready to hear the words. He let it go to voice mail.

***

After the funeral, Blake walked alone on the beach, just a few hundred feet away from St. Andrews Chapel by the Sea. Winter brought solitude and empty beaches to the Outer Banks. He welcomed the peaceful seclusion. A pair of seagulls, gliding overhead in search of food, squawked, letting Blake know he wasn't truly alone. A chilly, salty breeze blew through his hair. He stood with his hands tucked in his pockets as he stared out over the dark-blue water.

The waves rolled up to the shore drenching the sand. The night before, a strong storm whipped up the ocean. The surf had calmed, leaving a treasure trove of shells on the white sandy beach. As if the sea blessed the day for his family, the dark clouds rolled away, and the sun burned off the early morning fog, clearing the skyline. The wind still carried the pipe organ music that ushered his granddad's journey to his eternal resting place—the sea. On the chartered boat, three miles out in deep waters, the waves carried Granddad's ashes to the horizon, where the earth meets the heavens. After the scattering of ashes, mourners made their way back to the chapel. Blake remained on the beach. Alone, lost in his thoughts.

His mind swam through thoughts of happy childhood memories of his granddad and him surf fishing for red drum. He envisioned them waking hours before sunrise, getting to the beach at the break of dawn, and staking out rods in the sand —rods that were twice his height. Granddad was careful to space the lines out far enough, so the lines wouldn't get crossed, and then he taught Blake about baiting and working the lines for a catch. With his granddad as a fishing buddy, they never went home with an empty cooler. But today, he realized he reeled in more than a catch. Long ago, he'd reeled in memories that would live in his heart forever.

He remembered during the summers, before getting his driver's permit, being dropped off at his granddad's bait and tackle shop. Vacationers flocked to his shop. His granddad was an expert fisherman and became anglers' best friend. His shop was just a stone's throw away from the pier.

Blake smiled as he recalled how his granddad allowed Blake and his best friend take a bucket and go clamming. They'd wade out into the bay until the water covered them up to their waist and dig deep into the sandy bottom for clams. His granddad grew up in a time when no one worried about kids roaming along the shore by themselves, so he didn't worry about the boys. Still, he knew his daughter would worry, so they kept the free-range excursions to themselves.

In his early teens, Blake loved when his granddad let him stand at the wheel of his sailboat, *The Magnolia*, with strong and steady winds gliding the boat toward the horizon. When the winds demanded, Blake would shift the sails as lines slid through his hands.

Blake was more of a fair-weather sailor. He'd heard his granddad's tales of being caught in dangerous storms with ominous clouds rolling in as he tried to navigate the explosive combination of heavy winds lashing, stinging rain, swells rising, and lightening flashing across the sky. Many times, Granddad confessed, he wondered if it would be his last sail, and the ocean would swallow him up. But he always survived—he'd turn the boat around and race back to the safety of the port.

Granddad, like his ancestors before him, was a seafaring man, and the sea was his life. Today, his granddad became part of the sea.

A familiar voice interrupted his thoughts. It

stopped him in his tracks. Blake turned and saw his ex-fiancé, Karen. The shawl she wore around her shoulders to shield her from the chilly air flapped in the breeze. The heels she'd removed dangled in her right hand as her toes sunk in the cool wet sand. She was just as lovely and carefree as he'd remembered.

"Do you mind if I join you?"

He thought it would be rude to turn her away. Afterall, she'd come to show her respects to his family. "No, not at all."

Blake's hands still in his pockets, Karen slipped her arm through his. Just as they once did, they slowly strolled arm-in-arm down the beach, in casual conversation, catching up on their professional careers.

Karen bent down and picked up a small piece of driftwood and drew in the sand. "Do you remember?"

"Remember what, in particular?"

As she finished drawing a heart shape, she reminded him, "This is the exact spot where you proposed, and we wrote our names in the sand."

"Is it? I thought it was closer to the chapel," he answered nonchalantly.

"No, we walked away from the chapel. Maybe you originally planned to get down on one knee in front of the chapel but had to walk a bit to muster up courage."

He found the topic awkward. Blake wondered where this conversation was headed.

"That was a long time ago. No reason to take a trip down memory lane."

"But there is." She dropped the driftwood and faced him. She held his arm and pulled him closer—close enough to kiss. She drew him to her lips.

For a moment Blake responded—but only for a moment. He took a step back, breaking the embrace. "What's going on, Karen?"

"I'm here to tell you that I'm sorry. I made a huge mistake when I left you. I've never loved anyone like I did you." Her eyes begged for forgiveness. "I'm asking for a second chance. Can you give me that? Can we start over?"

His heart wounded from grief, he was in no condition to carry on this exchange, but he knew it was inescapable.

His eyes cast on the sea, and he stood in silence for a few moments. It seemed like an eternity to Karen. He may not have remembered the exact spot where he'd proposed, but other memories flooded his mind. He'd remembered she'd erased their love from her heart as easy as the water erased their names in the sand. He remembered the hurt, the betrayal, and living day-to-day to just get by. He remembered their fairy-tale plans of spending their lives together and when those best-laid plans had not turned out as he'd hoped. He also remembered the nights he'd lain awake thinking of her, wondering if he'd ever crossed her mind. But eventually, thoughts of her faded, and he'd moved on.

With raw emotions and a firm grip, he held her shoulders and looked straight in her eyes. He decided to speak truth to Karen. "I need to be painfully honest with you." He thought of the misery she'd forced upon him. He didn't intend to inflict pain, but he knew his words would cut deep. "There's no starting over. There's no *we* in the future."

It surprised her that he'd used her own words to silence her—to dissolve her hopes. "Well then, you've made yourself crystal clear." Her begging eyes transformed into flashes of anger. "I won't beg. I guess we have nothing more to say." Karen jerked away from him. She didn't like the finality but had to accept reality. As she walked back toward the path leading to the chapel, she looked over her shoulder. His back was turned as he wandered aimlessly. He'd rejected her. She grieved her past.

After the unexpected kiss, Blake sought higher and stable ground on a comfortable sand dune for his weak knees. The tall, spiky sea oats that surrounded him gave him a sense of privacy. He'd wished he hadn't been so blunt. It was touching that she came to express her sympathy, but she was the last person he'd expected to see at the funeral. After the memorial began, he saw her slip in the back of the chapel. He'd admit that something stirred inside him. When she didn't join the mourners for the scattering of the ashes, she'd slipped out of his mind. He certainly didn't expect that afterwards, she'd stick around and search him out. At one time, they'd planned a life together, but today, the kiss—she meant nothing to him. She'd betrayed him and broke his heart—even worse, she violated his trust.

When his knees were ready to support him, Blake rose to his feet and headed back toward the chapel. Alone again with his thoughts, Blake realized that he had never seriously considered his own future as a father or grandfather. But somehow, death brought to his mind the prospect of new birth—fathering. Today, he envisioned a young boy running the beach, in his hand a kite, flying higher and higher up to the sky. He could also see a little girl with hair blowing in the wind, walking hand-in-hand with her mother, beachcombing in search of the perfect shell.

Dark clouds blew back into shore, accompanied by a light rain. Courtney's words echoed in his thoughts; *I love listening to the voice of raindrops*. Remembering the night she spoke those words, he also remembered promising himself, *every time I hear the sound of rain, I'll think of Courtney*. He whispered out loud, "Every time I hear the sound of rain, I'll think of Courtney."

He hadn't expected the emptiness—the desperate way he was missing Courtney. He wondered if she, too, felt the aching loneliness. Before he'd left Spring Valley, from time to time, he'd sensed hesitation. He reminded himself of her hidden scars from domestic abuse and how the past had unrelenting power to keep a soul from moving forward. Blake believed God had a plan for his life and had crossed his and Courtney's paths— a divine appointment. If she would allow, he'd help her break the power of her past—begin again and cling to the hope for the future. Blake knew what he had to do. Karen was his past. Courtney and her children were his future.

His granddad had blessed Blake's life. Now, as a specific echo to that prayer, Blake prayed someday he would be a blessing to Gracie and Chance. It concerned him that Courtney hadn't responded to his text messages, calls, or voice mails. He hoped and prayed Courtney would be waiting for him in Spring Valley.

Chapter Twenty

Sleepy or not, she had a full schedule and had to get out of bed. She was emotionally and physically exhausted. The past week, Courtney had worked her three-day shift with the nurse practitioner that filled in for Blake during his family-emergency, made quick trips to the hospital to check on Ada, and ran the kids to play practice. As if these normal activities weren't enough, Courtney also completed a rescue mission by securing housing at the Haven House women's shelter for the woman whom they suspected was a survivor of spousal abuse when they had treated her injuries on the Health Bus. She and her child were now safe, but Courtney felt the emotional drain of that event. Courtney managed her daily mom duties, began Christmas shopping, and finished gathering gifts for their Giving Tree project that she and Blake were supposed to deliver the next evening. But, since she had no idea if or when he would return, she'd manage on her own. He hadn't bothered to tell her he was leaving, and after reading the note left for him at the inn from his ex-fiancé Karen, Courtney decided she was through with Blake. She didn't hear a peep from him the night he left or the following morning.

Then when he decided to call, she'd decided to not answer. She didn't even listen to the messages he left on voice mail. Why should I? she asked herself. If he didn't have the courtesy to let her know his plans from the beginning, she would afford him the same. She wouldn't allow him to break her heart. She was incredibly disappointed in him, but just as disappointed with herself that she allowed him a place in her life. She scolded herself. Had I been a fool to open my heart to him? How could I have let my guard down and fallen in love with him—allowed him to get close to my children? She was done with him—done with men. She'd reserve her heart and love for her children. After all, as a mother, that's where her heart lived.

Gracie was still wrapped in blankets snuggled up next to her mom. During the dark days of her past marriage, when Courtney would finally fall asleep, she escaped to a peaceful land, free of turmoil. Now, years later when her precious Gracie slept, sleep brought nightmares.

Terrified from the recurring nightmare, Gracie had crawled into her mom's bed in the middle of the night, clutching Misty, her Beanie Baby plush, stuffed snowman. This was occurring more times than Courtney cared to count. With each visit, she tried to get her daughter to open up and let her know what she dreamed, but each night Gracie would say she didn't remember. Tonight, she talked. As her mom held her tight, Gracie revealed her nightmare. In her dream she saw her mother struggling with a bad man trying to steal her purse while Gracie is hiding in a closet, peeking through the door. The robber runs out of the house, but Courtney has blood on her face and is wearing sunglasses in the house.

As she listened to her daughter, a knot tightened in her stomach realizing Gracie witnessed the final scuffle she had with Joshua when he'd tried to steal grocery money from her purse to feed his addiction, beating her in the process. At the time, she'd thought Gracie was in her room sound asleep. The scene must have been buried deep in her subconscious and surfacing in her dreams. Courtney remembered the advice Abby gave when she'd shared her concerns about Gracie's nightmare. As she gathered her thoughts, she prayed for wisdom. She felt there was no reason to tell Gracie the whole truth as Courtney calmed her fears, so she went with partial truth. She told her sweet daughter that she was probably remembering when there was a bad man in the house that tried to steal her purse. Trying to reassure her, she emphasized that she was safe, that her mommy, brother, and papaw wouldn't let anything happen to her. Then they prayed together asking God to take away the nightmares, trusting God to give them a blessing of peace and happiness.

Before Gracie closed her eyes, she asked her mother if Blake would also help keep her safe. Courtney couldn't answer that question. For all she knew, she may never see Blake again. She'd only told Gracie that Blake was out of town for a family emergency. "Honey, Blake doesn't live here. I don't know when or if he is coming back. But, I promise, I'll keep you safe." That was one promise Courtney would keep, and she would use her most powerful weapon as a mother, the power of prayer.

Courtney knew first-hand how audible prayers were a source of encouragement because of the supernatural feeling that came from praying over or with someone. Courtney remembered how praying was awkward at first. A lady in her small group at church gave her a little devotional prayer and promises book to help in her new prayer journey. It proved to help her connect with God and to believe in the promises of His word. In her darkest days, sometimes prayers and promises were all she had to get her through the day. Prayers and promises got her and Gracie through the night.

She'd met death when it visited and took her mother; Courtney was only sixteen and had never experienced such pain. She didn't know how to mourn or manage her grief. It took almost two decades to move beyond anger to acceptance, then forgiveness followed. When death came for her children's father, history seemed to repeat itself, as so often it does. But she knew their pain. She'd questioned God if her suffering as a teen paved the way for her to mother, to comfort her children through their journey of grief. She knew the answer—they'd shared in the fellowship of suffering and comforted one another.

***

With her mind on her Saturday to-do-list, she headed for the kitchen and straight to the cabinet entirely devoted to coffee mugs. She was glad that her dad saved her mother's coffee mug collection. When he'd remodeled the house as a guesthouse, he added the shelving and mug collection. Today, she chose the mug with the quote, "Coffee is a hug in a mug." Every time she held the mug, it felt as if her mother had her arms wrapped around her. She desperately missed her mother. In matters-of-the-heart, she'd know what to advise. She smiled thinking of her mom and how much she would have loved her grandchildren.

***

Standing on her porch lit with sparkling holiday lights, panic washed over him. He'd snatched people from death, one could even say he'd brough them back to life, and he'd traveled to war-torn countries to tend to the sick. In those circumstances, he'd always remained calm, but with his hand outstretched to knock on the door with the cheery snowman wreath, he feared the woman in the house might not welcome him with a cheery disposition and open arms. For a moment he hesitated. He could stay in Spring Valley or move on to another assignment, but he couldn't escape the fact that Courtney brought life and love back to his heart. He had to tell her. He had to know if she felt the same.

He knocked on the door. He heard Gracie yell out, "I'll get it!" In an instant, she wrapped her arms around Blake's legs in a welcoming bear hug. Still squeezing him she said, "I knew you'd come back. I just knew it."

He stood there with a lump in his throat, fighting back the tears.

"Mommy, it's Blake!" Gracie took him by the hand and led him inside, out of the cold.

"I'll be right there."

He couldn't judge the tone of Courtney's voice. He heard no implied invitation to make himself at home, just a straight forward announcement.

"Chance and Nick are decorating the houseboat for the boat parade on Lady Lake with Papaw Rich. It's just me and Mommy at home wrapping presents." Gracie noticed the gift bag that Blake carried. "Is that present for Mommy?"

Blake put his finger to his lips, "Shhh, it's a surprise. Would you hide it?"

Gracie pretended to zip her mouth and tucked the gift under the tree.

Rolls of colorful wrapping paper, tape, and ribbons were strewn over the dining table. A make-shift assembly line, with unwrapped gifts on one end and wrapped on the other.

Courtney entered the room from the hallway wearing skinny jeans and an oversized, ugly Christmas sweater that she made look beautiful. She and Gracie wore matching kitty slippers as cute as the real cat who swatted around the scrap wrapping paper that had fallen to the floor.

Blake spoke first, "I hope it's okay that I dropped by unannounced."

"You left unannounced. That seems to be your M.O."

Her sharp tone revealed her mood. He thought she should never play poker. "You're mad at me, aren't you?"

"I wouldn't say mad." With Gracie in the room, she needed to choose her words carefully. "I would say, I'm disappointed—greatly disappointed." She emphasized *greatly*.

Gracie was old enough to know when adults needed privacy to talk, and she desperately wanted her mom and Blake together. She picked up the cat and started walking toward her bedroom. "We're going to go play in my room for a while."

"Okay, sweetie, I'll come and get you to finish wrapping gifts when we're done."

Blake hoped those weren't prophetic words —*we're done*.

Courtney headed straight to the coffee maker. She needed caffeine to think clearly. "Want a cup?" For him, she chose the mug that read, "Decaf only works if you throw it at people."

He followed her to the kitchen, and when he saw the mug in her hand, he wondered if it was a warning. Maybe he should be prepared to duck and take cover. He didn't need these jitters; he was already anxious. "No, thank you. I wanted to tell you in person—"

She raised her hand to stop him. Her eyes narrowed. "If you've come to say you're leaving, don't bother, just go." She poured the fresh brew in the cup. "Don't make things any harder on me or my children."

"Courtney—"

"Just a minute, I have more to say." She leaned her back against the kitchen counter. Hurt and disappointment carried the conversation, pushing her anger almost to the point of tears. "It may have been rude for me not to pick up when you called, and I didn't bother to listen to your voice mail. After I read the message Karen left for you, I couldn't bear to hear your voice or your excuses. I understand the urgency of a family emergency. What I don't understand is why you didn't feel the need to call or text when you left. I thought we had a connection—a mutual respect for one another. I thought I deserved an explanation." She sipped her coffee—swallowed hard to gulp back the tears. "It's not just my heart I'm trying to protect. I have to protect my children."

She stopped, waiting for an explanation.

Blake's mind was racing. He had to take a minute to process Courtney's accusations. Since he just learned Courtney hadn't even listened to his voice mail, she didn't know his grandfather had died. He could only imagine what went through her mind. Plus, he had no idea how Karen's name had entered the conversation.

"You're right. I'm sorry for not calling you immediately. But in my defense, the call from my mother came in after midnight, informing me that my grandfather was on his death bed, and I needed to return immediately. I didn't want to wake you in the middle of the night. I knew the hospital would find a replacement for me and let you know." His eyes begged for forgiveness. "Within twenty-four hours after I left, I reached out time and time again, but you didn't reply."

She bit her bottom lip and sent him a sympathetic look. Her voice softened. "I'm sorry. I didn't know about your grandfather. I feel so bad now."

"It's been a chaotic and emotional trip. I'm sorry I disappointed you. I should have called on my drive home." He wanted her to embrace him, but she stood stoically across from him. "And I don't know anything about a message from Karen. It must have come after I left."

"The front desk received a message for you from Karen that said, I quote, 'I'm looking forward to seeing you on your visit home.'"

Those words played over and over, like a broken record, in her mind all week long. *I'm looking forward to seeing you.*

"For all I knew, your ex-fiancé Karen was your family emergency. From her message, I don't think that was too far of a stretch to imagine." Still fighting back her tears, she apologized. "I'm sorry that was the first scenario I imagined. I can't explain why—but that's what I thought."

He knew why—she'd experienced her trust being shattered by a man she'd loved before. Why would Blake be any different? He took a step erasing the space between them, and gently caressing her face, he confessed, "Karen showed up at my grandfather's funeral and asked for a second chance, but I told her I had no feelings for her, what we once had was gone, forever in the past and that I was in love with another woman."

Hearing those words, Courtney closed her eyes and hung her head in embarrassment. She had no right to accuse him of betrayal. She'd let past trauma take control of her thoughts and imagined the worst of him. The sinking feeling in the pit of her stomach—the guilt she was experiencing, signaled that she not only had let herself down but also let Blake down by unjustly accusing him of betrayal.

He gently lifted her chin. Without saying a word, his powerful eyes spoke forgiveness. He understood. He didn't pity her, but he conveyed loving sympathy for what she'd been through.

He gazed straight into Courtney's gorgeous eyes. "You are my future. You, Chance, and Gracie. I love you, Courtney Clark. If you'll have me, I'll love you forever."

"But what about your next assignment?

You have wanderlust in your DNA—remember?"

"I'm giving up traveling medicine. The nurse practitioner on leave has decided not to return. The hospital offered me the full-time NP position on the Health Bus. I'll accept it, that is, if you want me to stay."

She nodded, pressing her lips close together. "Yes! A thousand times yes!"

She lost the battle with tears, and Blake gently wiped them away. She threw her arms around his neck and hugged him. She felt secure, cradled in his embrace. He pressed his lips to hers. He pulled back to look into her eyes and to repeat, "I've fallen madly in love with you."

"I love you, Blake Boone."

Blake stepped away to gather the gift that Gracie had hidden for him under the tree and handed it to Courtney.

She reached in the bag and pulled out a coffee mug set. One mug had imprinted, "Let's Make Coffee Together." The second mug added, "For the Rest of Our Lives."

From feeling hopelessly heartsick in the morning to a proposal in the afternoon, joy flowed through her, and happiness danced in Courtney's heart. But she had to make sure she wasn't assuming anything. This security and love felt like a caffeine buzz, but way better. She held the mugs up. "Is this your way of proposing?"

He reached in his pocket for the diamond ring his grandmother gave him to use as an engagement ring. "The mugs and this." He took her hand and slid the ring on her finger. It fit perfectly. "Will you marry me?" Waiting for a response, he couldn't take his eyes off her. She was glowing.

"It's beautiful! It's perfect!"

"The coffee mugs or the ring?" He teased.

"Both. Yes! I'll marry you!" She wrapped her arms around him as they kissed.

From the back of the house they heard, "Can I come out now?"

Courtney and Blake laughed; she hugged him again.

"Yes, Gracie. You can come out now. We have something exciting to tell you."

Chapter Twenty-One

Blake awoke with a renewed sense of happiness, ready to face whatever the day's challenges presented. Whether it had been professing his love for Courtney or the decision to stay in Spring Valley, the anxiety and stress that accompanied his mind over the past few days dissolved in his sleep. He still held sorrow for the passing of his granddad, but he held to the hope and promise they would meet again.

He had breakfast delivered to his room, so he could finish his art project. Before he left to pick up Courtney and the kids, he added the finishing touches to his watercolor painting, mounting the painting to a wood panel and sealing the artwork with several coats of clear coat spray. He opened the window a tad to ventilate the room, and a cool breeze dipped the room temperature.

He was pleased with the gift he'd created for Courtney depicting her children playing in the snow on a wintry day. He painted Gracie busy building a snowman and Chance standing a few feet away with hand cocked back to rocket a snow ball at his little sister. He felt he'd captured Gracie's fun-loving personality and love for snowmen and Chance's mischievous big brother antics.

Christmas couldn't come soon enough; he could hardly wait to see Courtney's expression when he unveiled her gift. It was a painting of love.

***

She wanted to include her children in the delivery of the Giving Tree wish granting mission, so they would experience the joy of giving to those in need. Chance helped Blake load the Jeep with stacks of colorfully wrapped presents while Courtney and Gracie carefully packed the Christmas cookie decorating kits that Chef Jean provided.

It had snowed during the previous night, but the roads were clear for travel. They drove the familiar route with its twists and turns on the narrow mountain roads—the same winding road they'd taken on their first Health Bus trip together. A few days earlier, Colleen and Abby, from the Giving Tree wish granting crew, delivered the Christmas trees and twinkling lights to decorate the travel trailers, brightening a gloomy situation and representing Christ lighting the world. As they pulled into the church parking lot, Courtney smiled thinking how Christmas decorations had a way of bringing happiness and hope. These families needed both, considering the overwhelming sadness and trauma they experienced when the flood washed away all of their material possessions.

Everything went smoothly up until the last family. When Blake knocked on the door, he was greeted by an anxious man. Blake soon discovered the cause of the man's anxiety when he saw the very pregnant woman lying on the couch in full labor.

"My wife is about to deliver our baby. I don't want to risk driving and her delivering in the car on the way. I've called the ambulance, but I don't think the baby is going to wait, and I don't know what to do."

Blake informed him that he was a nurse practitioner and could deliver the baby. He calmly took control and accessed the situation, brought Courtney in for assistance, and assigned the two wide-eyed children in the crowded travel trailer to join Chance and Gracie in the church parking lot to build a snowman.

**

Absorbed in observing the labor and delivery task at hand, Gracie peeked through the window unnoticed. To get a better view, she'd climbed on a hay bale that provided insulation for under the trailer. She watched Blake and her mom begin helping the woman. Blake told her mom to grab towels and blankets. She put some underneath the lady and sat some aside. Gracie hid her eyes most of the time, but she saw that Blake and her mom had no fear when the woman screamed out in pain. When Chance heard the screaming, he told Gracie to get away from the window. She ignored him, she could only stare. She couldn't turn away. She wanted to see the baby. When Blake guided the baby out, it cried, and Courtney immediately wrapped a towel around the newborn. Gracie had always wondered how babies came into this world, and now she had her answer. She was amazed that in one moment the woman was crying out in pain, and the next moment, when the baby took its first breath and cried, the woman was all smiles and even laughed. Gracie thought she kind of understood because that's the way she'd been feeling. She'd been sad for a long time, but recently, her heart felt lighter, happier since Blake came to Spring Valley. He made her mommy happy. She smiled as she watched her mommy handing the newborn to its mother. To not be found out, Gracie hopped off the hay bale and sprinted toward the snowman to join the building crew.

***

While waiting on the ambulance, Courtney peeked out the door to check on the kids. The other children were enthralled in a snowball fight while Gracie worked in solitude finding rocks for the eyes and adding branches for the snowman's arms. Gracie looked happy. Happier than she'd seen her daughter look in a long time. As she watched, Courtney thought she would love to see the world through her daughter's eyes—escaping a chaotic world by playing, creating an imaginary snowman friend. Someday, she imagined, when Gracie held the title of Mom, she will see her children as her mamma does—and they will be a blessing.

There were miracles yet in the world,

Courtney reflected, because she'd witnessed a miracle tonight. She'd seen miracles work in her children's lives and experienced her own little miracle—a Christmas love story.

**

The medical crew arrived and safely loaded mom and baby in the emergency vehicle. The dad shuttled the kids off to a neighboring trailer, thanked Blake and Courtney profusely for their help, and then followed his wife and newborn to the hospital.

On the trip home, they'd stopped at McDonald's drive-thru to pick up a bite to eat. The kids were busy in the back seat munching burgers. Even though the nights became long and dark, December's Cold Moon was enchanting as it poured a brilliant silvery moonlight over the mountains.

"Do you think the full moon triggered labor?" Courtney looked over at Blake.

"If you read what the experts have to say, they claim lunar effect on labor and deliveries is a myth, but in my experience, births seem to increase dramatically during a full-moon shift."

"Appalachian folklore tends to rely on full moons. I heard my granny say leaving diapers on the clothesline during a full moon will attract evil forces."

Blake furrowed his brow. "That doesn't sound good."

"My papaw always said to plant crops under

a full moon for a bountiful harvest."

"That one sounds more reasonable."

"See what you think about this one," Courtney recalled. "You should spit on a new baby to bring it good luck."

Chance chimed in from the back seat, "That disgusting!"

"I'm with Chance. That's disgusting!" Blake winked in the rear-view mirror at Chance.

When the kids drifted off to sleep, Courtney kept reflecting on what she'd just experienced. "I think I have an idea of what the early mountain midwives felt when they traveled back into the remote hills on horseback to assist Appalachian women in labor and birth. They were called angels on horseback."

"When I took this assignment for the Health Bus, I read in the early days the midwives were associated with the Frontier Nursing University."

"Back in the day, in my grandparents' neck of the woods, Granny said the nurse-midwives equipped the saddlebags with their medical supplies, and when kids asked where babies came from, instead of the stork lore, they'd tell them the midwives' saddlebags." She chuckled. "Before the nurse-midwives, in the mountains we had 'granny midwives' who weren't officially trained but who attended to most births."

"I'm just trilled we practice medicine with the bus instead of horseback."

"Tonight was nothing short of incredible!"

"The cramped living space of the travel trailer made for a tight working space. But overall, the delivery went smoothly."

"Just so you know, you'll have to hire a new Community Health Navigator for the bus because I quit!"

Confused, Blake glanced over at Courtney and reached for her hand. "What do you mean, you quit? I assumed everything was good with us."

"Oh, it's better than good—it's remarkably good. I've been thinking about advancing my career. Tonight confirmed a new direction for me. I want to go back to school for a nursing degree and become a licensed Registered Nurse specializing in labor and delivery."

"From what I've seen, you'd be perfect in the field. Being an RN will definitely open up many different opportunities. But, I've got to be honest. I'll be sad that we'll not be working together."

"I would just be a distraction, anyway. You need to concentrate on your patients," she teased, giving his hand a little squeeze.

"You're right about that. When romance is in the air, it can be distracting. You sound so excited and happy, just talking about it. Know that you can count on my unconditional support."

"Somehow, I knew you'd be my biggest cheerleader. But, don't worry, I won't jump into it right away since we have a wedding to plan. But count on it; it's going to happen."

"I love you so much, and I will always be

your cheerleader. I believe in you. Whatever you dream, I'll help make those dreams come true," Blake declared.

His words had her heart leaping with joy. "I love you, and we'll dream together."

Courtney knew his words were more than flowery speech—they were a promise. A promise of love that would bind them forever.

***

An hour later, Blake found himself carrying a sleeping Gracie into the house. Chance helped his mom carry in backpacks and gathered the McDonald's wrappers for the trash.

"If you'll take her to her bedroom, I'll get her dressed for bed and tuck her in," Courtney whispered to Blake.

Blake laid her on the bed. As he turned to leave, Gracie opened her eyes halfway and said in a soft, sweet voice, "I love you."

"I love you, Gracie." His heart melted.

Courtney helped Gracie change into her pajamas and kissed her goodnight. As she snuggled her pillow, Courtney recognized the glow on her daughter's face because she saw it in her own reflection in the mirror earlier that morning. She was amazed that the pain and the sadness that had resided in their hearts and souls for so long was replaced by joy. A scripture came to mind that her granny used to quote: *We have this hope as an anchor for the soul, firm and secure.* It's true, she thought, we're never beyond hope and happiness.

Courtney tucked Chance in bed. Nick jumped on top of the covers to snuggle with his pal. "Mom, will you and Blake get married right away?"

Courtney knew that Chance painfully missed and mourned the death of his father because he held good memories of his dad before the drug addiction. Chance had slowly learned how to live life without his dad. He'd also taken on the big brother protector role for Gracie. Courtney and Blake's whirlwind romance happened so rapidly. Gracie had an immediate bond with Blake, but she realized it may take more time for Chance to adjust.

"Sweetie, we haven't set a date. We wanted to include you and Gracie in the planning."

"That's a good idea. I'm sure Gracie will want to be the flower girl." He grinned imagining his little sister skipping and giggling while attempting to hold a basket and scatter petals at the same time. "I really like Blake; I just don't want to forget Dad."

Courtney bent down and kissed Chance on the forehead. "Don't you worry. I'll never let you forget your dad." She put her hand over her heart. "He'll always live in your heart." As she switched off the lamp on the nightstand, she assured Chance, "Just understand that Blake is not a replacement for your dad, but I know he loves you and Gracie and will love and support you as if you were his own children."

Chance's eyes misted over. "Blake is really cool. Would you tell him I said so?" He reached for the corner of the sheet and rubbed his eyes, wiping away the tears. "I'm happy that you're getting married."

Courtney reached over and playfully mussed his hair. "I'll tell him. And just so you know, you can talk to me about anything. I promise I'll always listen."

Chance shook his head in agreement and patted his fur baby on his head. "Good night, Mom. I love you."

"I love you, my sweet boy."

Courtney knew as she and Blake planned their lives together, she'd seek professional advice on forming a new blended family. Courtney was so wrapped up in her emotions that she reminded herself to be extra sensitive to the upcoming challenges and changes in her children's lives.

She found Blake on the couch. She sat beside him, curled her legs up under her, and then turned to look into his eyes.

"Chance thinks you're cool, and Gracie is quite smitten with you."

Blake ran his finger down her cheek. "Good, because I'm smitten with this whole family."

He drew her to him, gently kissed her forehead and then her lips.

"I better get back to the inn."

He rose, and she stood to come with him, fingers interlaced.

He stood at the door, turned to frame her face in his hands, and once more kissed her goodnight.

She went to the window, pulled back the curtain, and waved goodbye. She was happy.

Chapter Twenty-Two

Monday night, after practice for the play, The Year of the Perfect Christmas Tree, Blake promised treats from the Mockingbird. They walked up the hill from the Spring Valley theater into the coffee house filled with the warm and cozy aroma of the season wafting through the shop, a blend of coffee, sugar, vanilla, and cinnamon. The perfect combination for the festive holiday mood. They were surprised to find Ada and J.R. enjoying coffee and dessert at a table.

Courtney bent down and gave Ada a hug. "You look incredible!"

"I feel incredible! I convinced J.R. to bring me to the coffee house if I promised I'd be a customer and not the boss."

"She's having a hard time keeping her promise," J.R. interrupted. To be honest, he was just glad she wanted to get out of the house and enjoy some company.

"I just had to be here, if only for a few minutes. It's my little sanctuary." She closed her eyes for a quick moment, smiled, and took a deep breath. Ada invited, "Get your drinks and dessert and come join us. There's plenty of room."

Courtney thought Ada's face glowed with her new lease on life. "We would love to if you're sure the kids won't bother you. After they get their cocoa and sugar fix, I can't expect good behavior."

"They'll be fine!"

"Okay, we'll be right back."

They returned with an array of decadent desserts. Gracie and Chance chose gingerbread man cookies with the s'mores hot cocoa, Courtney had the peppermint mocha and a slice of chess pie, while Gabe went for the Hummingbird Cake and their special Christmas coffee blend.

"I heard you had some excitement during your Giving Tree delivery." Ada couldn't wait to hear the full story from the source.

"Delivery is the operative word. "Blake shared the experience, leaving out the gory details since the children were present.

Gracie listened and pretended she didn't see a thing while her brother gave her the side-eyed look, desperately wanting to tattle-tale on her but kept his mouth shut.

Courtney turned and looked at Blake. "Is it always going to be like this with you? Heart attacks and emergency deliveries?"

"Practicing medicine, I've come to always expect the unexpected." He shrugged his shoulders and smiled.

"You two either have impeccable timing or bad luck follows you," Ada laughed. "No, I'm just kidding. From my point of view, you two are angels of life. Always coming to the rescue of someone in need. You kept me walking on this earth and in a moment's notice helped bring a new life into this world. I am in awe and wonder."

"We have other exciting news." Courtney subtly held the coffee cup handle at the perfect angle, so the diamond ring would catch the light and sparkle, and she excitedly announced, "We're engaged!"

"Oh my! It's beautiful! Bless your hearts." Ada held her hand close to her heart. You two are the perfect match!" Ada watched as Blake lovingly gazed at his fiancé. "Courtney, you've always said that you wanted someone to look at you the way you look at coffee. I think you found your man."

"I agree." Courtney leaned over and kissed Blake.

Chance, still at the age of thinking kissing is gross protested, "Eww! Do you have to kiss in front of us?"

Gracie giggled and encouraged another kiss, "Smooch! Smooch!"

Sitting next to Gracie, Ada cuddled her up close and asked, "Gracie, what do you think about Blake and your mom getting married?"

Gracie wiped the whipped cream off her lip with her sleeve. "I love it! I prayed that Blake would marry Mommy."

"Oh, my goodness! Do you know what answered prayers are called."

"No, what?"

"They're called blessings, and this answered prayer is your Christmas blessing."

Gracie smiled. She remembered whispering her Christmas wish to Santa, wishing Blake could be her dad and make her mommy happy. Santa said that wish wasn't in his department. It was something called a blessing, and she needed to pray about it. Santa was right! She was so happy; she wanted to dance around the coffee house like a sugar plum fairy. She nibbled on a delicious arm of the gingerbread man cookie and sipped her cocoa imagining skipping down the church aisle, throwing flower petals at her mommy's wedding.

Ada loved inspiring little ones to pray. She lived a life of prayer. To her, prayer was as natural as breathing. When she prayed power prayers of blessings on the lives of those she lifted up in Spring Vallely, the heavens opened up and poured bountiful blessings. Surrounded by love, she silently prayed, "Lord, bless this little family."

Ada's heart may have been weak from her heart attack, but she felt strong and reinvigorated. She was three for three in her matchmaking endeavors. Blake and Courtney added another precious love story to her hobby. They were a romance made in heaven. She decided she'd ignore J.R.'s request to give up her matchmaking *pet project*. She knew that her Lord was the supreme matchmaker that forged the path, but the romantic in her loved a good love story, and she enjoyed being a part of Divine dates.

Happiness sparkled inside her as she held her cup to toast the happy couple. "There's just something miraculous about Christmas when love is in the air. To Blake and Courtney!"

Clinking their mugs in unison, they cheered, "To Blake and Courtney! Merry Christmas!"

THE END

Be happy and full of joy because the Lord has done a wonderful thing.

Scripture Reference

The Lord bless thee and keep thee.
Numbers 6:24

He will not forget your work and the love
you have shown him as you have helped
people and continue to help them.
Hebrews 6:10

Perfume and incense bring joy to the
heart, and the pleasantness of a friend
springs from their heartfelt advice.
Proverbs 27:9

You will be blessed when you come
in and when you go out.
Deuteronomy 28:6

"A Samaritan, as he traveled, came
where a (wounded)man was; and when
he saw him, he took pity on him".
Parable of the Good Samaritan
Luke 10:29-27

"Today, in the town of David a Savior has been

born to you; he is the Messiah, the Lord. This
will be a sign to you: You will find the baby
wrapped in cloths and lying in a manger."
Luke 2:11-12

"Look at the birds of the air; they do not sow
or reap or store away in barns, and yet your
heavenly Father feeds them. Are you not much
more valuable than they? Can any one of you
by worrying add a single hour to your life?"
Matthew 6:25-27

Pray in the Spirit on all occasions with all kind of
prayers and requests. With this in mind, be alert
and always keep praying for all the Lord's people.
Ephesians 6:18

"Now is your time of grief, but I (Christ)
will see you again and you will rejoice, and
no one will take away your joy."
John 16:22

Let my teaching fall like rain and my words
descend like dew, like showers on new grass,
like abundant rain on tender plants.
Deuteronomy 32:2

The God of all comfort, who comforts us in all our
troubles, so that we can comfort those in any trouble
with the comfort we ourselves receive from God.
2 Corinthians 1:4

We have this hope as an anchor for
the soul, firm and secure.

Hebrews 6:19

*And God is able to bless you abundantly, so that
in all things at all times, having all that you
need, you will abound in every good work.*
2 Corinthians 9:18

*"They are always generous and lend freely;
their children will be a blessing."*
Psalms 37:26

*"And he (Jesus) took the children in his arms,
placed his hands on them and blessed them."*
Mark 10:16

*"Then Jesus told him,"Because you have seen
me, you have believed; blessed are those who
have not seen and yet have believed.""*
John 20:29

*"The Lord bless you and keep you; the Lord make his
face shine on you and be gracious to you; the Lord
turn his face toward you and give you peace."*
Numbers 6:24-26

Blessed are the pure in heart, for they will see God.
Matthew 5:8

*The Lord has done great things for us,
and we are filled with joy.*
Psalm 126:3

About The Author

A Note From Georgia

A big heartfelt thank you for reading A CHRISTMAS BLESSING FOR GRACIE! I hope you were blessed by Courtney and Blake's story and found it to be an inspirational love story that illustrates how the chance of love and a Christmas blessing is possible with the help of faith and divine intervention. These strangers, each searching for happiness and true love that lasts, were brought together during the season of miracles. I pray for God's special Christmas blessing on you and yours.

If you did enjoy the novel, I would love for you to write a review. Reviews are a tremendous help to authors and I would love to read your feedback. It's also a great help for readers interested in one of my books for the first time.

You can post a review on Amazon or go to my website and leave a review message, sign up for New Releases in 2024 and Blog Posts:

www.georgiacurtisling.com

If you haven't read the entire Spring Valley Series, be sure to check out THE ORNAMENT OF HOPE and SANTA'S PROMISING CHRISTMAS. You'll love them!!

Thank you and Christmas blessings!
Georgia

-Spring Valley Heartwarming Romance Series –
The Ornament of Hope
Santa's Promising Christmas
A Christmas Blessing for Gracie

About the Author

GEORGIA CURTIS LING
Born and raised in the foothills of the Appalachian Mountains, Georgia holds dear the three inherent mountain values of faith, family, and the land. Her Spring Valley series, including The Ornament of Hope, Santa's Promising Christmas and A Christmas Blessing for Gracie are rich with voices from the past, memories of heartwarming stories, and traditions of her cherished heritage. She and her husband, Phil, live in central Kentucky, just a few hours' drive from their son, Philip, and daughter-in-heart, Lauren.

Georgia is the bestselling author of What's in the

Bible for Women, Mom's Lead in Love, and In Mom They Trust. She touches the heart and tickles the funny bone as she writes about faith, love, and life. Over her career, her work has appeared in numerous periodicals and nine bestselling books.

For new release dates go to:
www.georgiacurtisling.com

SAMARITAN'S PURSE
Join me in supporting Samaritan's Purse U.S. Disaster Relief. The 2022 round of flooding in the Appalachian region was the worst flooding in the region's recorded history. In eastern Kentucky, floods claimed 39 lives and inundated hundreds of homes under feet of water. Samaritan's Purse relief teams immediately responded to the disaster acting as the hands and feet of Christ. Samaritan's Purse mobilizes and equips thousands of volunteers to provide emergency aid to U.S. victims of wildfires, floods, tornadoes, hurricanes, and other natural disasters. In the aftermath of major storms, Samaritan's purse often stays behind to rebuild houses for people with nowhere else to turn for help.
To donate, go to: samaritanspurse.org

Made in the USA
Las Vegas, NV
20 October 2023

79411434R00136